Books by Stephen Krensky

A
Ghostly
Business

A
Ghostly
Business

by Stephen Krensky

Atheneum *1985* *New York*

Library of Congress Cataloging in Publication Data

Krensky, Stephen.   A ghostly business.

SUMMARY: While visiting their Aunt Celia in Boston,
the five Wynd children are determined to foil the
army of ghosts intent on helping an unscrupulous
developer acquire some of the best property in the city.
Sequel to "The Dragon Circle" and "The Witching Hour."
[1. Ghosts—Fiction. 2. Magic—Fiction] I. Title.
PZ7.K883Gh 1984   [Fic]   84-2971
ISBN 0-689-31048-X

Published simultaneously in Canada by
McClelland & Stewart, Ltd.
Composition by
Dix Typesetters, Inc., Syracuse, New York
Printed and bound by
Fairfield Graphics, Fairfield, Pennsylvania
Designed by Mary Ahern

3 5 7 9 11 13 15 17 19 F/C 20 18 16 14 12 10 8 6 4

7460

For Joan

A
Ghostly
Business

ONE

THE BOSTON BUS station was a busy place that Thursday evening in December. Departing passengers checked their belongings in a giant clog of confusion while arriving ones exchanged hugs and hellos with welcoming committees of every shape and size. Among the less conspicuous arrivals were the Wynd children from Westbridge, Massachusetts. The five of them—Alison, Edward, Jamie, Jennifer, and Perry—had just stepped off the bus, and they were waiting to reclaim their baggage.

"I thought the trip would never end," said Perry.

His older brother, Jamie, smiled. "It was noisy at first. That guy was snoring up a storm. How did you make him stop, Jennifer?"

"I used a little spell to take away his voice.

He got the sleep he wanted, and everyone else got peace and quiet."

This explanation did not surprise the others. In a family where magic was as common as breathing, a silence spell was nothing special.

"I'm glad we're finally here," said Alison. "I've been looking forward to this trip."

Jennifer snorted. "Every year we visit Aunt Celia during Christmas vacation, and every year you say the same thing. But it's not the traveling you like, it's the shopping."

"Is that so?"

Jennifer nodded. "Shopping's like a disease with you."

Alison tossed her head. "That's the kind of opinion I expect from a twelve-year-old. When you're sixteen, you'll think differently."

"Anyway," said Edward, "this year will be different for us all, now that Aunt Celia's moved to the city."

"I wonder what her new house is like," said Jamie.

Perry sighed. "Whatever it's like, it won't have room service."

"You'll bear up somehow," said Edward, who had never shared Perry's love for ordering hamburgers after midnight. "And remember what

Father said before we left. He thinks Aunt Celia's been a little depressed since she moved. We're supposed to cheer her up."

With their luggage in hand, they entered the waiting room.

"Does anyone see her?" asked Alison.

"I hope she didn't forget," said Jennifer. "She is pretty absent-minded."

"Stubborn, too," said Jamie. "Remember last Fourth of July at the carnival? She insisted that the Tilt-a-Whirl only went clockwise. I explained that the cups spun both ways. She wouldn't listen." He shook his head. "But when she went for a ride, her cup only went clockwise. The guy running the machine couldn't believe it. He kept rubbing his eyes."

"Great Aunt Celia doesn't use her magic much," said Edward. "But when she does, it's best to be paying attention."

"I see her!" said Perry. "Over by the window."

"Oh-oh," said Edward, turning pale.

The others followed his glance. Aunt Celia was standing in a corner of the terminal, dressed as always in clothes that had been fashionable during the early 'Fifties. Having found a style she liked thirty years before, she had stuck with

5

it ever since. The children were used to this, though. What concerned them now was something else.

Aunt Celia was not standing on the floor of the terminal. She was floating three inches above it.

Waving and shouting, the Wynds descended on their aunt, hiding her feet from view.

She blinked happily at them.

"Oh, here you are!" she exclaimed. "I was expecting you, wasn't I? Of course, I was. Why else would I be at the bus station? There might be another reason, but none comes to—Children, children, I'm glad to see you, too, but you needn't tug so. I'm not going anywhere."

They could see that. Edward and Alison had hoped they could lower Aunt Celia without mentioning the matter. That wasn't going to be possible.

"Aunt Celia," said Perry, "do you know where your feet are?"

"At the end of my legs, I hope." She looked down. "Yes, there they are."

"But have you noticed what's under them?" asked Edward.

She glanced down again. "Goodness, I seem to have uprooted myself. Perfectly understandable, though. It was hard to look for you in all this hubbub. I thought the extra height would help."

"But what if you were seen?" said Jennifer.

"Goodness, child, people have better things to do in bus stations than look at other people's feet."

"Now that you've found us, though . . ." said Jamie.

Aunt Celia nodded. "I see your point." With a brief sigh, she settled to the ground.

The children looked relieved.

"I suppose we can all . . ." Aunt Celia frowned. "That man certainly is making an awful racket."

They all turned around. A man in rumpled clothes, clutching a suitcase in one hand, was banging on the counter for the clerk's attention. Once he had it, he pointed to his mouth and made gasping sounds.

"Jennifer," said Edward, "isn't that . . ."

"Ooops!" she cried. "I forgot all about him." Tracing a circle in the air, she tossed it toward the commotion.

". . . you idiot! Can't you see I've lost my voice? I'm not mad. I—" The man glanced around, suddenly aware that he could hear himself shouting. And if he could hear himself, then the people staring at him must be able to as well.

"The president of the bus line shall hear of this," he declared. Then he stalked away.

The clerk shrugged. In his job he saw all kinds.

Jennifer had a more select group of people staring at her. "So I forgot," she said. "It could happen to any—"

"Dummy," Perry finished for her.

Aunt Celia frowned. "If that man had been wearing a scarf, this wouldn't have happened. People just don't take proper care of themselves anymore."

"I hope you weren't waiting for us too long," said Edward, thinking it best to change the subject. "The bus from Albany was a little late."

"Albany? Have you moved to Albany? Why doesn't anyone tell me these things."

"We haven't moved," Alison assured her. "That's just where the bus starts. We got on in Westbridge."

"Smart of you not to move," their aunt declared. "There's been enough moving in this family at present."

"We're looking forward to seeing your new house," said Jamie.

Aunt Celia hesitated for a moment. "And I'm looking forward to showing it to you," she said.

AUNT CELIA had always maintained that she would never live in a home younger than she was. Clearly with her new one she had many years to spare. The house had stood for almost two centuries, resisting the changes that had inevitably come to the neighborhood. Larger apartment buildings adjoined it, and amid these Victorian giants, the house seemed to be fighting for elbow room. Its slate roof was cast in almost perpetual shadow, and its brick front looked undernourished next to the substantial masonry of its neighbors.

"How beautiful," said Jennifer through the taxi window. The others echoed her view.

Aunt Celia brightened. She paid off the cab, unlocked the door, and led the way inside.

The children spilled into the hall.

"Nice high ceilings," said Edward.

"Look at that bannister!" cried Perry. "It's a lot steeper than ours."

"No bannister rides tonight," said Alison. She glanced around. "Aunt Celia, you look very settled here. The clock . . . the hutch . . . the sideboard. Your furniture fits in perfectly." She noticed something odd, though. It looked as if someone had started sprucing up the place, and then simply stopped before the job was done. A silver bowl in particular caught her attention. Half of it gleamed, while the other half was still covered with tarnish.

Aunt Celia had also noticed the bowl. She squinted at it, and then pottered over for a closer look. "I don't remember doing this," she murmured, tracing the edge of the polish with her finger. "Obviously I did." She shook her head. "I've been very tired since the move."

"Don't worry," said Alison, "We'll help you get the place in order. Won't we, guys? Guys?"

"Oh, sure," said the others.

Aunt Celia sighed. "Thank you. I know that will help."

Jennifer shivered.

"Are you cold, dear? I can turn up the heat . . ."

"No, I just thought I felt something." She shook her head bewilderedly.

"Probably scared herself looking in the mirror," muttered Perry.

Jennifer shrugged. "It's gone now."

"Just as well," said Alison. "It's too late in the day to start overworking your imagination."

"Possibly a lingering chill," said Aunt Celia, stroking Jennifer's hair. "You had a long trip. You'll feel better once you're settled in."

There were three guest bedrooms on the second floor and a small attic one on the third. Perry claimed the latter—it would give him the best lookout, he said.

"What are you on the lookout for?" asked Alison.

"Sea monsters."

"Oh," Alison never argued with Perry about things like that.

"Edward and Jamie can share the large front room," said Aunt Celia. "Jennifer can have the other. Alison can have the back bedroom opposite mine. Now, children, you get unpacked, and I'll make some sandwiches in the kitchen. After your long ride, you must be starving."

By the time they returned downstairs, a platter of sandwiches was sitting on the kitchen table. Aunt Celia was busy at the stove, taking a steaming saucepan off the burner.

"Cocoa all around?" she asked.

Everyone nodded.

She began pouring the hot milk into mugs.

"Shouldn't we add something?" said Edward.

Aunt Celia waved a magical hand at him. "I just did," she bubbled. "Drink up, drink up."

It was true that the milk had changed color. Alison took a cautious sip. "Aunt Celia," she said, "this doesn't taste exactly like cocoa."

"No? What does it taste like?"

"Milky tea."

Their aunt took a sip from her own mug. "So it is. Too much top spin, I guess. My wrists aren't as supple as they once were. Jamie, there's cocoa in the cupboard behind you. We'll make some in a more conventional way."

The phone rang.

Aunt Celia picked up the receiver. "Hello? Yes, this is Celia Wynd. Oh, it's you, Mr. Ratchet . . . No, I haven't changed my mind . . . Yes, I know how generous your offer was. But I told you before, it isn't a question of money." She sighed. "Yes, I still have your number if I change my mind. Goodbye."

She cradled the phone. "That man certainly is persistent. He's called three times this week."

"Is he a crank?" asked Perry.

Aunt Celia smiled. "Oh, no, he's just doing his job. Mr. Ratchet represents some real estate interests. Quite the wheeler-dealers, I gather.

They want to renovate the apartment building next door. But their plans involve joining that building to one on my property."

Perry snorted. "There's not much room here for apartments."

"There is if they tear the house down and build something higher and more modern in its place."

"Would they do that?" said Jennifer.

"I'm afraid so, dear. It happens all the time. But I have no plans to sell."

CRRAASSSH!

"What was that?" said Jamie.

"It came from the front hall," said Edward.

They all rushed out of the kitchen. There in the hall, by the feet of the sideboard, the punch-bowl was wobbling on the floor. Alison picked it up. The bowl was brighter than before. More of the tarnish was gone.

"Aunt Celia, were you trying a cleaning spell on this? You shouldn't strain yourself like that. We said we'd be glad to help out, and we meant it."

Aunt Celia was blinking repeatedly. "A cleaning spell? I didn't conjure one. At least I don't remember . . . Could I do it without knowing I did it? Or could I do it and then forget?" She shuddered. "I think I'm getting a headache."

She wandered back into the kitchen.

The Wynds just looked at one another. Keeping an eye on Aunt Celia was likely to be more difficult than they had thought.

TWO

EDWARD woke up early the next morning. He dressed quietly, so as not to wake Jamie, or at least he tried to.

"What are you doing?" mumbled his brother. The bottom half of Edward was sticking out from under the bed.

"Looking for my boots," came the muffled reply. Edward wriggled back out into the open air. "Sorry I woke you. I'll look later." He tiptoed from the room in his socks.

Edward was not alarmed about his missing boots, but he did wonder who had taken them. Jennifer was the likely culprit. After all, he had spoiled her cooking experiment the week before. Edward was all for advancing the frontiers of science, but he had feared for everyone's safety when Jennifer had started mixing those two steaming beakers together. Grabbing them from her hands and pouring their contents out the window had not been polite, but it had removed the direct threat of an explosion. Jennifer, however, had not shared this view. The missing boots were possibly part of some complicated plan of revenge. Jennifer was very big on complicated plans.

With no disturbances to wake him, Perry slept later. When he did awake, he shuffled over to the window seat and looked out at the rooftops. A ship's cabin would be like this, he thought, with exposed beams and sloping walls. The windows were a little large, perhaps, but when you were a battle-weary sea captain grabbing a few moments rest on a long voyage, the size of the portholes didn't matter.

Outside the window and down the block, the cars were honking at one another. To Perry, it was the sound of gulls gliding in and out of the ship's sails. The ship must be nearing land. The captain checked his uniform in the mirror; he wished to look his best when he went ashore. The captain passed a finger over a scar that ran the length of one cheek, a souvenir of a duel five years before. It was said that the scar grew fiercely red in the heat of battle, but the captain had never verified this for himself.

There was a knock at the door.

"Enter."

Jamie came in. "Are you up, sleepyhead?"

Perry waved a finger at him. "I advise you to show more respect for your captain, Lieutenant. Such familiarity is bad for discipline."

"Oh?" Jamie was used to this. Perry often became a pirate captain at a moment's notice. He had probably spent half of his nine years sailing the high seas in his bedroom. "Captain, I crave forgiveness. I don't know what got into me. A touch of fever, perhaps."

"On your knees," said the captain. "Maybe then my temper will cool."

"But your majesty," said the lieutenant, isn't craving forgiveness enough?"

"You dare to mock me? On your knees, dog, and be quick about it!"

"Never," said the lieutenant, who had a stubborn streak as wide as the deep blue sea. "I have my pride, Captain."

"Then look to your pride to defend you." Drawing his sword from his scabbard, the captain lunged at his junior officer.

The lieutenant parried the blow and returned one of his own. Back and forth they went at it, their sabers moving so fast that a bystander might not have seen them at all.

ain soon began to get the worst of it. ...enant had the edge in size and ... and he forced the captain back against ...k.

...eld!" cried the lieutenant.

"Hah!" the captain sneered. The lieutenant might have the brawn, but it was he, the captain, who had the brains. Reaching out with his free hand, he came upon a pillow and raised it over his head.

"So, Captain!" bellowed the lieutenant, "you would waste a bottle of your best port on me."

"Aye," said the captain, throwing it at his opponent.

The lieutenant ducked, and the port hit the wall behind him. He picked it up.

"A sturdy bottle," he marveled, "not to break after a blow like that. And now it will serve my purpose as well as yours." He made ready to throw it back.

Perry was prepared for that. As Jamie wound up, the pillow exploded, showering Jamie in a flurry of feathers.

"No fair, Captain," sputtered the lieutenant. "You used sorcery on me."

The captain was too busy laughing to argue the point. And the lieutenant soon joined him.

They were still picking feathers out of Jamie's hair when Edward poked his head through the doorway.

"What are you two doing up here? It sounded like a herd of elephants dancing a jig." He folded his arms. "Let me guess. No doubt I just missed the further adventures of Captain Perry and his touchy first mate."

"Boy, Edward," said Perry, "I hope I'm not such a grump when I'm old like you."

"Fifteen isn't old. It's mature."

Jamie shuddered. "You mean I've only got one happy year left before"—he clutched his chest —"maturity takes over."

Edward ignored him. He shook his head at the scattered feathers. "Maturity is what makes you think twice before you start destroying property. Tell me, how do you plan to explain about the pillow to Aunt Celia?"

Neither the captain nor his first mate had an answer ready.

"That's what I thought," said Edward.

"The whole thing's here," Perry insisted. "We'll just have to put it back together."

"Well, not now. I came up to get you for breakfast. Then we're going shopping. You can clean this up later."

"Yes, Admiral," said Jamie, darting out the door before Edward could grab him.

UNLIKE the others, Jennifer was still trying to sleep. She was very dedicated when it came to getting enough rest, and on vacations her dedication knew no bounds. The sun might stream in through the window, voices might pass on the stairs, but she would do her best to ignore them.

When the air suddenly turned cold, though, she couldn't ignore that. She shivered and pulled the blanket around her. It didn't help. She was growing wider awake by the second. Finally she opened one eye.

"It must be a draft," she muttered. Sticking a finger in her mouth, she held it up to the air. There was no breeze to speak of, but the coldness remained. Where was it coming from? Falling out of bed, Jennifer began to circle the room. She almost tripped over some boots—Edward's, she realized—without wondering what they were doing there. She was more concerned with the draft.

It was the coldest near the closet. Opening the door, she looked in.

Everything seemed perfectly normal. Her clothes were innocently hanging on their hangers, and some boxes were minding their own business on the shelves above them.

And the feeling of cold was gone.

Jennifer frowned. How was that possible? Bitter colds didn't just come and go at will. She knelt down and inspected the walls. Maybe there was an old chimney or some hole that was only partially blocked up. She checked the baseboards and had begun poking at the molding when the cold returned from behind her. She turned to get up, and the closet door slammed shut.

"Hey!" she shouted, "I'm in here!"

Nobody answered, but she could hear something being pressed against the door. She tried turning the doorknob. It wouldn't budge. It was jammed from the other side.

"All right," said Jennifer, "you guys have had your little joke. Don't push your luck. Perry? Jamie? Come on, open up."

Her plea went unheeded.

"Very well," she said, "no more Mr. Nice Guy." Whatever was jamming the door rattled when she shook the knob, so it couldn't be too heavy. Jennifer placed her hands on the knob, fashioned a spell, and pushed.

Something landed with a clatter in the middle of the room. The doorknob came loose, and Jennifer threw open the door, expecting to find one of her brothers laughing at her.

But nobody was there. The chair that had been propped against the doorknob was now lying on its side near the bed. Otherwise, the room looked undisturbed.

"Hmmmph!" grumbled Jennifer. "They may think leaving the scene of the crime will help. But I'll track them down, and when I do, they'll be sorry."

When she found the others, though, they looked anything but sorry. Mostly they looked hungry, which was why they were eating breakfast.

"Sleeping Beauty gets up at last," said Perry.

Jennifer glared at him. "It wouldn't be wise for you to make things any worse."

"Keep your voice down," said Alison. "You'll disturb Aunt Celia."

Jennifer shut the kitchen door. "I want to know who's responsible," she said. "Which one of you locked me in the closet?"

Perry giggled. The others looked at her in surprise.

"Well, Perry?" Jennifer demanded.

"Don't look at me like that. It sounds like a good idea, but I had nothing to do with it."

Jennifer was not impressed. "You can't all be innocent. At least one of you—"

"Before you get launched," said Edward, "can you tell me when I can expect my boots back?"

"Your boots?"

"That's right."

Jennifer paused. "They're in my room."

Edward folded his arms. "And how did they get there?"

"How should I know? They're your boots."

"I suppose you had nothing to do with it," said Jamie, grinning.

"Nothing to do with what?"

Edward stood up. "I'll go get them. I'll be back in a minute."

Perry shook his head. "Pretty clever, Jen, I'll admit that. Waltzing in here with this closet story—it makes a good diversion. But it won't work."

"Don't diversion me, Perry. The smart money is still betting on you. Where were you fifteen minutes ago?"

Perry smiled. "Here," he said.

"Can you prove it?"

"We've all been here for about half an hour," said Alison.

"Oh?" Jennifer frowned. Alison would never

cover for her brothers. It was a time-honored rule in the Wynd household that if you wanted to give lumps, you had to be able to take them, too.

"So much for your accusations," said Jamie.

Jennifer looked confused. "I think you should still hear what happened," she said. "I—"

"Maybe later," said Edward, pushing open the door. He held out the boots in front of him. Parts of them were polished, others remained scuffed. The laces were covered with goop.

"Now about these boots . . ."

When Edward put on his serious voice, Jennifer knew she was in trouble. The only problem was, she hadn't done anything.

"I don't know how that happened."

"Hah!" said Perry.

"Better to own up now," Jamie cautioned her.

Jennifer was getting mad. "You're crazy," she said. "The first time I saw those boots today was when I got out of bed. I almost tripped over them."

"Talk is cheap," said Perry. "What else can you say in your defense?"

"I'm innocent until proven guilty." Jennifer looked at their faces. "Or am I?"

"We really should iron this out," said Alison.

"Iron it out yourselves," said Jennifer. "You weren't interested in my story. I'm not interested in yours." And true to her word, she opened the door and left.

"Whew!" said Jamie.

"If she was acting," said Edward, "that was quite a performance."

"Don't be fooled," said Perry. "She took the boots. What other explanation is there?"

Nobody had one handy, but that didn't help much.

THREE

WHEN Aunt Celia came looking for Jennifer to see what she wanted for breakfast, Alison explained that Jennifer had gone for a walk.

"A daily constitutional, eh?" Aunt Celia nodded approvingly. "That's the way to keep in shape. Mark my words, Jennifer will return relaxed and refreshed."

"Let's hope so," said Alison. "I, ah, doubt she'll be back before we go shopping. We'll catch up with her at lunchtime."

They soon left the house. As Aunt Celia led her merry band across Boston Common, they passed some children having a snowball fight.

"Ouch!" exclaimed Jamie.

"What's the matter, dear?" asked Aunt Celia.

Jamie shook out his scarf. "I was just hit with a snowball."

"Just an accident," said Alison. "No big deal."

The boy responsible was about to call out an apology when his friend stopped him.

"They're just tourists," she said. "Don't bother." She snickered. "Look at the way they dress . . . What a joke."

A second boy scrutinized the departing Wynds.

"Bet you can't hit that hat."

"Bet I can," said the girl. "Watch."

The hat in question belonged to Perry. It was a stocking cap, knitted to his exact specifications by his mother. The red, brown, and yellow hat might not be the height of fashion, but Perry liked it.

A snowball whizzed through the air, nicking his ear.

Perry whirled. The boys were laughing. Perry took a step forward, but Edward grabbed his arm.

"That was no accident."

"Forget it, Perry. We don't want to make a scene."

The boys hooted.

"Chicken!"

"That hat isn't the only thing that's yellow."

A second snowball hit Edward in the shoulder.

Jamie ducked as a third snowball came his way.

"We're not here to start trouble," Alison reminded them. "We can just walk on. There's no need to—"

A snowball hit her in the face.

"On the other hand," she said, wiping the snow from her forehead, "sometimes you have to make a stand. Sometimes people have to be taught a lesson."

"I'm all for that," said Perry.

Aunt Celia straightened her coat. "I'm glad to see you showing some sense," she declared. "Of course, we are outnumbered . . ." She scooped up a handful of snow. "That should make it interesting."

The others followed her lead.

The local children couldn't believe their eyes.

"Go home before you get hurt," said one laughing. "You're in the big city now."

"We'll take our chances," Perry shouted back.

The boy grinned. He had a dozen friends with him. The big mouth only had four, and one of them was an old woman. They wouldn't aim at her, of course, but the others would be fair game.

"Ready!" said Perry.

"Aim!" said Jamie.

"Fire!" said Aunt Celia.

Five snowballs flew through the air.

"Hits?" asked Alison.

"Two hats and two arms," Perry reported. "And Aunt Celia knocked a snowball out of the big kid's hand."

The local children were surprised that so many snowballs found their marks, but even strangers could have a little dumb luck. Now it was time to return the fire. These tourists would be sorry they had ever gotten up this morning.

A dozen snowballs flew across the yards of neutral ground. They were well-aimed, but that hardly mattered. As the snowballs neared their targets, they crumbled into powder and blew away.

"Fire at will!" Edward declared.

For the local children, the contest quickly became a nightmare. Their snowballs all fell short or exploded in the wind. But the tourists never seemed to miss, and their shots had an uncanny knack for hitting arms and hats or destroying ammunition piled on the ground.

Perry was trying to model his throws on Aunt Celia's delivery. She wound up like a baseball pitcher, releasing her snowball with blazing speed.

"Where'd you learn to throw like that?" he asked.

"Fenway Park," she replied, unloading a pitch that knocked one boy into the girl behind him. "When I go to a baseball game, I pay attention."

"How about one at a time?" said Jamie.

The others nodded.

Now each of the local children was hit with five snowballs at once. They ducked as best they could, but somehow the snowballs seemed to duck with them. The old woman's throws were the worst. Her blows stung long after the others had faded. The children had never faced anything like this, and they didn't know what to do.

The Wynds began to advance, and their foes fell back to a new position. But what started as an orderly retreat soon became a full-fledged rout. Perry and Jamie chased them for a while to make sure they didn't regroup and come back.

Aunt Celia briskly rubbed her gloves together. "My, that was fun," she said.

"You're a great shot," Edward said admiringly.

"Even so, Aunt Celia," Alison felt obliged to add, "should you really be exerting yourself like that?"

"Of course. It's good for the circulation. I haven't felt so stirred in a long time." She smiled briefly. "I don't seem to be myself since I moved. You saw that punchbowl last night . . . All kinds of things have been going on." She shook her head. "I even thought I saw . . . No, no, I can't tell you. It's too ridiculous."

"You can tell us anything, Aunt Celia," said Edward.

"We've seen plenty of strange things in our time," Alison reminded her.

Aunt Celia considered for a moment. "Never mind. Forget I mentioned it. I was just rambling a bit . . . Ah, here come the boys. We can be off again."

THE CROWD near the wharf spilled over the sidewalks into the street. People were passing in and out of bookstores, record stores, shoe stores, department stores, and restaurants. Most of them were in a hurry, most of them were ladened with bags, and most of them wished they were home with their feet up.

"This city keeps changing," marveled Aunt

Celia. "Always a new building going up. It wasn't so long ago that you couldn't give away this property. Now there's a condominium on every corner. Horrible word, condominium. Sounds like some sort of radioactive element discovered in a lab.

"Look at that construction across the street. Patriot Center, they're going to call it. Do you know why? It's built on what was the Patriot Tavern. A fine old place, that was. It had quite a history. Should have been designated a landmark years ago. Now it's too late."

"Did you go there?" Perry asked.

"Not for many years. Decades ago Grace Salisbury used to take me there after a performance. She was in musical comedies, then." Aunt Celia shook her head. "Time goes by so fast, and we keep destroying all record of its passing." Her eyes focused on the camera around Edward's neck. "Is that camera just a decoration or do you plan to use it? I want memories of this day. I want pictures of you all."

"Do we have to?" said Perry. "Everyone will think we're tourists."

"Well, we are," said Alison.

"Your opinion doesn't count. You love having your picture taken."

"There's no crime in that."

"Well, then," said Perry, changing tactics, "I'll be happy to take the picture."

"It's my camera," said Edward. "I'll do the clicking."

"Not so," said Aunt Celia. "I want us all in the picture. Just put the camera down on that ledge over there, Edward. I'll do the rest."

Alison gasped. "Aunt Celia, you can't do that."

"Certainly I can, dear. I know the right spell."

"But people will see . . ."

"You think they would notice?" She paused. "I suppose you're right. A pity. Very well, Edward, you take it."

"Where should we stand?" asked Jamie.

"Bunch up together right where you are," said Edward, backing away. "Everyone smile. Perry, no rabbit ears on Alison. Okay, hold that. One more step back . . . Ready? One . . . two . . ."

Edward snapped the pictures in a hurry.

Jamie snorted. "You're not even aiming at us."

"Are you all right, Edward?" asked Aunt Celia.

Edward sighed. "They're gone now." He put the camera down.

The others turned to follow his state. All they saw was the sign heralding the arrival of Patriot Center.

"Who's gone?" asked Alison.

"What did you see?" asked Perry.

"I saw three men . . . It sounds silly . . . They were very pale and dressed in old clothes, I mean real old, like the Civil War or something. One looked like a sailor. But the strangest part . . ."

"Yes?" said Jamie.

"When they reached the fence around the construction project, they simply walked through it."

"Through?"

Edward nodded. "As if it wasn't even there."

"It could have been the sun playing tricks," said Alison.

"Or the power of suggestion," said Jamie. "Aunt Celia was talking history."

Aunt Celia looked thoughtful. "Yes, yes, I was, wasn't I?"

"You don't have to believe me," Edward snapped. "I have proof. Just wait till my pictures are developed."

"I'll wait," said Perry, "but I won't hold my breath."

WHEN JENNIFER returned to the house, she found a note explaining where everyone was. It was fine with her. She would stay home and sulk. Settling into a chair, Jennifer stared at the pendulum in the grandfather's clock. Her head swung slightly, matching its rhythm until she began to feel dizzy.

She squeezed her eyes shut—and suddenly froze. Were those footsteps she heard upstairs? Had someone else not gone shopping?

"Who's there?" she cried.

As soon as she said this, Jennifer felt a little dumb. It was only natural to hear strange noises in an old house. A place like this would keep up something of a racket just to maintain its self-respect.

The footsteps sounded again.

Jennifer tensed. Self-respect or not, she had never heard of a house that walked. She reviewed a few spells in her mind. If there was a burglar upstairs, he would rue this day for a long time.

The footsteps were directly overhead. That would be my room, Jennifer thought. Maybe the intruder hadn't heard her cry out. If not, she would still have the element of surprise. Step by step, she climbed the stairs. Was that the closet door being opened? Was this a clothes burglar? The idea was new to Jennifer, but you might find anything in a big city like Boston.

She crept along the hall. The noises had stopped, but whoever had been in the room must still be inside. There was no other way out.

Taking a deep breath, she threw open the door.

"All right," she said, "the party's over."

She was speaking to an empty room.

Jennifer checked the window. It was locked from the inside. There was nothing under the bed or in the closet. The room had no other hiding places. Jennifer frowned. Had she imagined the whole thing?

Footsteps overhead answered the question for her. Who was this guy? Houdini? Shaking her head, she tiptoed up to Perry's room. The narrow attic stairs creaked with every step. If the burglar had ears, he would know she was coming.

Unlike her own room, Perry's had an open door. Jennifer first checked behind it. Nobody was there. This room was empty, too. It smelled faintly of furniture polish, but was otherwise much as Jennifer expected. Since Perry had already spent one night here, the feathers scattered about did not surprise her. With Perry, anything was possible. It was strange, though, that the bed was half made. Perry made his bed only under the threat of death or worse. What would have prompted him to start on it?

Jennifer sighed. She was finding herself asking far too many questions. This was supposed to be a vacation. Clearly it was fast becoming something else.

FOUR

WHEN JENNIFER heard the family come in, she didn't get up. She was sitting in the living room, a book open in her lap. Her plan was to appear distant and preoccupied. It was a fine thing, she told herself, when your own family practically called you a liar. If that was the way they wanted to be, who needed them?

"Anyone disappear before your eyes on the way home?" Perry was asking in the hall.

"I saw what I saw," Edward maintained. "They walked through that fence. Wait till you see the pictures."

Jennifer couldn't help hearing this. Who had walked through a fence? What pictures? Her curiosity undid all her resolutions.

"Walk through a fence?" she asked, joining the others. "Who? When? How?"

"Don't get him started again," pleaded Jamie.

"Started about what?"

Alison explained.

Jennifer's mouth hung open. "I wish I'd been there," she said regretfully.

"Don't tell me you believe him," said Jamie.

"I don't know. I've been having my own experiences with someone walking through walls. Wait till I tell you . . . When I came back this morning, I heard footsteps upstairs, but—and this is the weird part—I couldn't find anyone to go with them."

Aunt Celia had not joined in the earlier exchange, but she spoke up now. "Now, dear," she said, her hands fluttering nervously, "do you really think that's possible?"

Jennifer was definite. "It's not only possible, it happened."

The phone rang.

Aunt Celia answered it. "Hello? Why, hello, Grace . . . Yes, yes, they arrived. Of course, I recognized them . . . No, they're right here in front of me. Yes, I remember. Dinner tonight, seven o'clock. What's that? No, it's a surprise. Yes, we'll all be here. 'Bye."

She cradled the phone.

"That was Grace Salisbury. I invited her for dinner tonight. She's eager to see you all again."

"That's nice," said Jennifer. "Now about those noises—"

"Later, dear. I should start cooking at once. Grace appreciates a good meal." She headed for the kitchen.

"But we should—" began Jennifer.

Alison touched her arm. "Don't push it," she advised softly. "Can't you see Aunt Celia is avoiding the subject?"

"Why would she do that?"

"Remember what happened last night with the punchbowl? I think Aunt Celia suspects herself of being responsible."

"How could that be?" asked Jamie.

Alison wasn't sure. "Maybe she's lost control of her magic. She was always absent-minded. This could be something worse. You saw how sensitive she was."

Jennifer frowned. "But this happened while she was out. Besides, what I heard didn't sound like spells on the loose, it sounded like an intruder. I think we should investigate."

"How?" asked Edward.

"Well, we should . . . we could . . . search the house," she finished lamely.

"If you couldn't find the source of the noises while they were being made," said Alison, "how would we find them now?"

"Assuming there really is something to find," said Jamie. "Old houses do creak, you know."

"I'm telling you there's an intruder . . ."

Even Edward found this hard to believe.

Perry laughed. "This family's got invisible people on the brain. You can look for them if you want. I'm going upstairs to put my stuff away."

The others followed his example, leaving Jennifer to fume in private.

Perry, however, took only a glance at his room before he returned downstairs.

"Ah, Jamie, can you come up to my room for a minute?"

"What for?"

"You'll see."

"A mystery, huh?" Jamie grinned at Edward. "It's just one thing after another around here."

But when he saw Perry's room, his smile faded. "What have you been doing up here? How come half the feathers are picked up and the other half aren't?"

Perry sighed. "I don't know. It looked like this when I came up."

"But when we left . . ."

"I know."

Jamie wrinkled his nose. "Do you think Jennifer was right? Could someone have been here?"

Perry sighed. He hated to think Jennifer could be right about anything. "I guess I'm not sure," he said.

WHEN the doorbell rang, all the children went to answer it. They had washed up and changed their clothes since lunch. Aunt Celia wanted them to look their best for company. Perry's best meant wool pants, and he hated them with a passion. They always made him itch.

Jamie opened the door.

"Celia!"

"Grace!"

Aunt Celia was addressing a large woman accompanied by a fox terrier. The two of them trotted into the house, leaving the children with the choice of giving way or being knocked down.

They gave way.

"You're looking very well, Celia."

"So are you, Grace. Here, let me take your coat."

As Aunt Celia reached out, the dog began to bark. He was a small fox terrier, but what he lacked in size, he made up for in voice.

"It's good to see you, too, Hector," said Aunt Celia.

Hector growled. There was something about this woman he didn't understand, and Hector was not the sort of dog who enjoyed being confused.

"Hector, behave yourself," said his lord and master.

The dog paused, but only long enough to catch his breath.

"Grace, you remember my nieces and nephews. From right to left, this is Perry, Edward, Alison, Jamie, and Jennifer."

"Hello!" they chorused.

"Fine looking family, Celia," said Grace.

Hector barked at Perry. Obviously he did not share this sentiment.

"Well, come in, come in," said Aunt Celia.

As they entered the living room, Jennifer shivered. That feeling of cold, the same one that had awakened her that morning, brushed the hairs on her neck.

"Some cheese and crackers, Grace?"

"That would be very nice."

Aunt Celia picked up the tray. "It seems the children have prepared these in advance." She offered the tray to her guest.

Grace took a cracker, and found her fingers meeting amidst the cheese. The cracker had been broken in several places.

"Excuse me," she said, wiping her fingers on a napkin.

Aunt Celia examined the tray closely. "I believe all the crackers are cracked." She smiled. "The children bring plenty of enthusiasm to helping out."

"It doesn't matter," said Grace, popping another cracker in her mouth. She chewed and swallowed. "They taste the same in any event." She breathed deeply. "And it certainly whets my appetite for what's to come. There are some intriguing smells coming from your kitchen."

Aunt Celia looked pleased. "Grace is a gourmet cook," she explained.

Miss Salisbury laughed. "What your aunt means," she told the children, "is that I like to eat. Of course, one look at me tells you that. When it comes to cooking, I'm my own best audience." She breathed deeply again. "Curried chicken, right?"

Aunt Celia nodded. "It should be almost ready. I'll just go check on it."

"I'll give you a hand," said Grace.

They left the room together.

Jamie shook his head. "Curried chicken? Why do people have to ruin things by covering them with goop?"

"Curried chicken is special," said Alison, "something Miss Salisbury will appreciate."

"Goop is goop," Jamie insisted.

"Never mind that," said Edward. "I want to know who messed up the crackers. It wasn't funny."

The others knew nothing about it.

"We all know it wasn't funny," said Alison. "We wouldn't pull a stunt like that on Aunt Celia."

Edward hadn't considered this. "Maybe not," he admitted, "but surely the cheese didn't spread itself."

"No," said Jennifer, "but . . ." She shivered. "The cold . . . Don't you feel it?"

They didn't.

"Look at Hector," said Perry.

The dog had marched over to the fireplace. He was barking up the chimney.

"Hector, stop that!" Miss Salisbury called from the kitchen.

Hector hesitated, then began yapping some more. Something very strange was going on in that fireplace, and he was not a dog to let it pass without notice.

Aunt Celia reappeared in the doorway. "Dinner is served," she announced.

The meal began smoothly for everyone except Hector. He refused to leave the living room fireplace, and he refused to stop barking, either.

"I apologize for Hector's manners," said Grace, sitting down at the table. He's not usually like this." She smiled at the gleaming china and silver. "This house reminds me of my grandmother's home. It was a very proper place. There were upstairs maids, downstairs maids—"

"Milkmaids?" asked Perry.

"You'll have to excuse him," said Jennifer. "He mistakenly thinks he has a sense of humor."

Grace beamed at Perry. "Don't apologize for him. We could have used a few more jokes like that in vaudeville."

"At one time Grace was quite a star," Aunt Celia put in. "Worked her way up from the chorus."

"I tried to get your aunt to join me," Grace confided to the children. "She was a great hoofer in her prime. But I couldn't convince her to try it."

At this point Hector appeared in the doorway. He was backing his way into the dining room, as though retreating from a menacing opponent. He was barking fiercely now.

Grace clapped her hands. "Come here, Hector!"

Hector looked toward her and then back to the hall. He didn't move.

"How strange," said Grace. "He's never disobeyed like this before."

"Perhaps he's showing off for us," said Aunt Celia. "Is everyone done with the soup? Then I'll bring in the chicken. Jamie, Edward, come help me with the rice and vegetables."

The boys left the table.

Jennifer felt a draft on her neck. She looked up and gasped. No wonder Hector hadn't moved. An old man was standing in the doorway. His skin and his clothes were gray and faintly glowing. Most upsetting of all, Jennifer could dimly see through him to the hall beyond.

However startling his appearance, the man did not seem dangerous. His expression mingled hesitation and puzzlement. Hector was keeping him at bay, and while the dog didn't actually attack, the man kept his distance.

Alison had followed her sister's gaze. She was openly gaping. So was Perry.

Miss Salisbury twisted around in her chair. "What are you all staring at?" She looked into the hallway and saw nothing. "Hector, have you gone mad?"

"Here we are," said Aunt Celia, taking slow measured steps from the kitchen. Edward and Jamie were right behind her. They were laughing about something, but their smiles froze as they too caught sight of the unexpected visitor.

"Aunt Celia . . ." began Alison.

Hector was trotting back and forth in front of the sideboard. His barking filled the room.

Aunt Celia was concentrating on getting the platter of chicken to the table. She looked up at Alison's call, though, and in doing so, she saw the man, too.

"Ooooh!" she exclaimed.

The platter of chicken fell to the floor.

"Goodness!" said Grace.

Hector stopped barking abruptly. The man was gone.

Grace was out of her chair at once. "Are you all right, Celia? I'm so sorry. I don't know what to say. I can't imagine what got into Hector. There's no excuse for him startling you like that."

Aunt Celia was waving her hand in front of

her face. "It's warm in here, isn't it?" She looked down. "I thought the recipe had turned out fairly well." A piece of chicken fell off her sweater. "I guess you'll have to take my word for it. Should we send out for pizza?"

"Don't worry about that," said Grace. "Let me help you get cleaned up."

As they left, the children looked around in silence. The only sound came from Hector. Having done his duty, he was contentedly mopping up the fallen chicken.

"You can't blame the dog for barking," said Jamie. "He thought he was protecting us."

Edward smiled grimly. "But protecting us from what?"

FIVE

S O NOW you're singing a different tune."
The delegation facing Jennifer was doing its best to look contrite, apologetic, and sorry. Perry was having a hard time keeping this up. In his view she was milking this for more than it was worth.

"We said we were sorry," said Alison.

"Eight times," Jamie noted.

"Nine," muttered Perry.

"All right," said Edward, "we should have listened to you when you told us about the intruder."

"And before that?"

"We shouldn't have assumed you had anything to do with my boots. We made a mistake. We admit it, and we feel bad about it."

"You should," said Jennifer.

"Okay, okay, but if the situation had been reversed, would you have done any differently?"

A small part of Jennifer wanted to insist that she would have; the other parts knew better. "Very well," she said, "apology accepted."

"I'm glad that's settled," said Alison. "In a way I'm relieved things have turned out this way. It's much better than thinking Aunt Celia was responsible, that magic was leaking out of her somehow and doing things on its own."

"Well, she certainly didn't invent that man," said Jamie. "He gave me the creeps."

"It's good Miss Salisbury didn't stay long," said Alison. "Did you see Aunt Celia's face? No wonder she went upstairs to lie down."

"Shouldn't we have told her that we saw him, too?" said Perry.

"The best thing for her now is rest. We can fill her in later when we know more."

"I wonder where he went," said Jennifer. "He could still be in the house, you know."

"How can we find out?" said Jamie. "Where should we begin looking?"

No one had a particularly good place to start. The children split up, Perry and Edward taking the top two floors, Jamie, Alison, and Jennifer searching the first floor and the basement.

An hour later, the children met again in the kitchen. There was no need for anyone to ask how the others had done. Their faces told the story.

"It's too bad Hector's gone," said Alison. "He could probably lead us straight to him."

Edward frowned thoughtfully. "Maybe Hector can still help us. Remember what he was doing just before Miss Salisbury took him away?"

"Eating," said Perry.

"After that. He stood here in the kitchen . . ."

"Barking at the cupboards," said Alison.

"Maybe he knew something we don't," said Edward. "Jennifer, do you feel any more drafts? From what you were saying, you seem especially sensitive to the intruder's presence."

Jennifer shook her head. She felt nothing.

Perry glanced warily at the walls. "Maybe there's a secret passage here somewhere."

"This isn't a castle, you know," Alison reminded him.

Perry was staring hard at the cupboard. "Do you notice something funny about those shelves?" he asked.

"Like a hidden door?" said Jamie, grinning.

"You can make fun if you want, but don't

those shelves look like they're framed by a doorway?"

Now that Perry mentioned it, the shelves were bordered by the same kind of framework that supported the doorways.

"There could be some kind of button or lever," he said.

They pressed and prodded all along the wall, hoping to activate a hidden mechanism.

They didn't.

Perry sighed. "I guess that would have been too easy," he muttered.

"Should we try somewhere else?" asked Jamie.

"Don't give up on this place yet," said Perry. "I'll bet Alison could open it."

Alison didn't know any spells for finding secret passages, but she was the family expert when it came to unlocking doors. The shelves and the wall behind them made a rather unconventional door, but that was only a technicality.

"I'm not sure . . ." she began.

"Come on," said Perry, "we've got nothing to lose. And Hector hasn't let us down yet."

Alison sighed. "Very well," she said.

There were old-fashioned spells and modern ones, spells with keys, spells with combinations, and spells that would remove the pins from hidden hinges. There were even spells that would open a door as though it had been kicked in.

Alison tried them all.

Finally, she stopped for a rest. "Either I'm losing my touch or there's no door here to open."

Perry wasn't prepared to accept this. "I say we investigate further. I still trust Hector's judgment."

Edward and Alison disagreed. They didn want to start taking Aunt Celia's house apart on a wild goose chase. It wasn't logical.

"Perry's right," said Jennifer. "We've already done the logical searching. It got us nowhere. We can be careful about this. The shelves can be put back as good as new."

"What do you say, Jamie?" asked Edward.

He smiled. "I say any idea that Perry and Jennifer agree about must have some merit."

Alison laughed. Jamie was right about that.

"All right," she said, "But we'll have to work together on this. Perry, pull those two chairs over here. You and Jennifer stand on them, and put your hands in the top corners. Edward, you stand in the middle with Jamie. All of you be ready to add a magical push to my spell."

The children took their places. Alison stepped

back and began the incantation. The edges of the shelves began to glow.

"Press on the corners," she told Perry and Jennifer.

A crack appeared in the paint covering the framework. It was not a jagged crack, but a perfectly straight line that cut at right angles in the four corners. The crack widened with each passing second, and as it did so, the glow brightened

"Now, push!" she said.

Edward and Jamie leaned against the shelves. For a moment the shelves remained still. Then, slowly, they began to move. The whole structure silently rolled inward like it was riding on wheels. Once it had cleared the inner wall, Alison brought it to a halt.

Beyond the shelves was a dimly lit room. It had once been some kind of pantry. There were glassed-in shelves on two walls, and a long counter and cabinets underneath. As interesting as this would have been at another time, the children's attention was focused on the far wall.

The intruder was sitting in a chair reading a book. He looked comfortably at home, but not peaceful exactly. When he turned a page, his gray hand shook. In the darkened room, he glowed more brightly than he had earlier.

The man seemed unaware that he was being

watched. He continued to read as the Wynds advanced on him.

"Hello," Alison said tentatively.

The man stiffened. He put down the book and looked around. He had an open face, his wrinkles and high forehead adding dignity to his owlish expression.

"We mean you no harm," said Jennifer.

The man did not look frightened, but his astonishment held his face rigid.

"You really can see me?" he said.

They nodded.

"And hear me?"

They nodded again.

"I thought I was imagining it before. Extraordinary, truly extraordinary." He sighed. "You're the first people I've spoken with in over eighty years."

"We are?" said Perry.

"Eighty years?" said Jennifer.

"A long time," the man acknowledged. "But it seems most people can't see ghosts."

"Ghosts!" the children cried.

He winced at their outburst. "There's no need to shout. Just because there's not much to me" —the ghost poked at his wispy stomach— "doesn't mean I'm deaf." He frowned. "By any chance are we related?"

"What's your name?" Edward asked.

"Baldridge. Henry Baldridge."

The children shook their heads. There were no Baldridges in the Wynd family tree.

"Odd," said Henry. "I've been told only close descendants could see a ghost, and not even all of them can manage it." He eyed the children sharply. "What makes you so different?"

"We, ah, have good eyesight in my family," said Edward. "We eat lots of carrots."

The ghost nodded. "The current master of the house, can she see me, too?"

"Of course," said Jamie.

"She has seen me before," Henry remarked. "On the day she moved in, I was dusting the mantle in the parlor." He looked embarrassed. "She looked right at me and muttered something about not giving in to senility. Obviously I had distressed her. It is not my function to do that, and I have avoided her presence ever since."

"But you still take a hand in the household affairs?" guessed Alison.

"Why, you're the one who polished my boots!" said Edward.

"And returned them to my room by mistake?" said Jennifer.

"Never dwell on the past," Henry declared.

"You were the one who tried to clean up the feathers . . ." said Perry.

"I was interrupted . . ." Henry explained.

"By me," said Jennifer. "But you're also the one who locked me in the closet."

"You were so sensitive to my presence, I got flustered. Don't you ever get flustered?"

"Were you flustered when you spread cheese on the crackers?" asked Jamie.

"And scared Hector to death?" said Alison.

Henry shuddered. "The dog was not frightened. I was."

"How do we know you're a ghost?" said Perry. "You don't look like a bedsheet."

"Real ghosts never do."

"Don't you rattle chains or scare people?"

Henry stiffened. "I do not engage in such pursuits."

"What do you engage in?" asked Jennifer.

"I serve," the ghost replied. "I was once the family butler here. This"—he indicated the room around them—"was once the butler's pantry. It was walled up during some renovating in the 'Thirties."

Jennifer was confused. "You're a butler, you say?"

"That's right."

"But a butler has to carry trays and open doors and all sorts of stuff. How can you do that and walk through walls, too?"

"You mean," said Henry, "how can I hold a book in one hand and pass my other hand through this table?"

He proceeded to demonstrate.

Jennifer gulped. "E-exactly," she said.

Henry smiled. "The choice of being solid or not at any given moment is mine to make," he said. "A small consolation for my current state, but something nonetheless."

Perry crossed his arms. His image of ghosts was undergoing a severe upheaval. It was hard for him to accept. "If you're really a ghost," he said, "that means you're dead, right?"

"Eighty-seven years ago next month." Henry paused. "It was a Thursday, I believe."

"You remember the day?" marveled Jamie.

"It's not the sort of day I'd be likely to forget."

"Eighty-seven years . . ." Edward repeated. "That fits with your clothes, but not with the way you talk. Shouldn't you sound a bit more, well, old-fashioned?"

"I may be a ghost," said Henry, "but I don't live in a cocoon. I keep up fairly well. It takes time, but I'm a rich man where time is concerned." He sighed, and the resulting blast of cold air chilled the room considerably.

"But how did you end up here in the first place?" asked Alison.

"Because of the curse," the ghost said simply.

"A curse!" the children exclaimed.

"That's right. Not a very complicated curse, just an effective one."

Jennifer could hear the sense of injustice in his voice. "Don't you worry," she said. "We'll help you get rid of it."

"I'm not worried," Henry insisted, rising to his feet. He had his pride to consider. "I can manage perfectly well on my own."

"Like you did with dinner?" said Jamie.

"The dog unsettled me. I admit I'm a little out of practice. My timing will improve."

"There's no harm—" began Alison.

"The matter is closed," Henry said firmly.

And before anyone could question him, he had walked through the wall, effectively ending the conversation.

SIX

THE OFFICES of Ratchet Real Estate, Inc. had lately moved from humble basement quarters to a group of suites on the fortieth floor of a downtown skyscraper. It was a move particularly relished by Horace T. Ratchet, the president of the firm. He was a small, beady man with darting eyes and four strands of hair covering an otherwise bald head. He cherished those strands dearly.

Horace Ratchet loved everything about his new office: he liked the big windows, the leather furniture, the thick carpeting—he even liked the music in the elevators. The rent was costing him a pretty penny, but pennies he now had in sackfuls. Horace Ratchet had recently become something of a legend in the real estate field. Long considered a slimy worm who would sell the Atlantic Ocean to any buyer who needed the water badly enough, Ratchet had suddenly become a shrewd and alert investor. Buildings that unexpectedly came on the market at distressed prices found him a ready and eager buyer. The properties were varied, but they all shared one thing in common: they had mysteriously lost their sound reputations. The owners were unwilling to discuss this in detail, they simply wanted out. And Horace T. Ratchet was always willing to oblige them.

His latest project, the expansion of an apartment building on Beacon Hill, was snagged at present. The hitch could be summed up in two words—Celia Wynd. Her purchase of the townhouse adjoining the property was holding up everything. Ratchet had offered the former owner more money than this Wynd woman had, but her bid had been accepted anyway. Money wasn't everything, the former owner had said. He didn't want the house destroyed.

Horace Ratchet snorted. A man with as little sense as that should have been put away.

He leaned back in his chair and put his feet up on his desk. It was too bad this Wynd problem would not go away by itself. He buzzed his secretary to get Celia Wynd on the phone The time had come to apply a little more oil

"Miss Wynd? Horace Ratchet, here. Just thought I'd check back with you. Have you given any more thought to my proposal . . . Yes, yes, I appreciate your feelings. But have you considered all the advantages? We know what you paid for the house. We're willing to give you a healthy profit for the time you've spent there." It pained Ratchet to say this, but he forced himself. "What?" The real estate magnate blinked incredulously. "You say a profit doesn't interest you. Come now, Miss Wynd, surely you're joking."

It was hard enough for Horace Ratchett to propose giving someone else a profit, but to be rebuffed in the effort was more than he could bear. He was not a patient man to begin with, and sparring with this stubborn old woman was fraying what little forebearance he had.

"I'm sure we can still . . . Oh, you will think about it. I'm pleased to hear that." Horace Ratchet looked up, and hastily pulled his feet down from his desktop. "Ah, you'll have to excuse me, Miss Wynd. I just remembered I have a meeting . . . It's been nice talking with you. We'll continue this discussion later. Goodbye."

"Who was that?"

The voice uttering this remark nicely matched the grim visage of the visitor standing before Horace Ratchet's desk. The voice was not the only noteworthy thing about Ephraim Skags. There was the gray color that uniformly covered his skin and clothes, the style of clothing itself, which had been out of fashion for almost a century, and the fact that a fairly good view of Boston was visible right through him.

"You really shouldn't just pop in like that. Couldn't you make an appointment?"

Skags did not smile. "Your secretary cannot see or hear me."

Ratchet had forgotten that. It wasn't easy dealing with a ghost when you were a busy man. But when that ghost was your great-great grandfather, and he was helping you get rich, you made allowances.

"Who was that?"

Ratchet made a face. "Celia Wynd."

"Has she broken yet?" Skags asked.

"No, but I think she's weakening."

Skags' eyes narrowed. "Only weakening?"

"Otherwise things are going very well," Ratchet said hastily. "Our plan—"

"Our plan?"

Ratchet adjusted his tie. "*Your* plan is working perfectly."

"So it is. But I no longer wish to undertake all

of the work myself. I want to expand the operation."

"Expand?" Horace Ratchet grinned. Instead of renting office space, he might soon buy his own skyscraper. The Horace T. Ratchet Building—it had a nice ring to it.

"You're woolgathering again," said Skags. "Pay attention. It's time to clean up loose ends before the big push. We've tried your approach with this Wynd woman. Now we'll try mine. I'll have some of my associates speak with Henry Baldridge. He's the ghostly butler in that house. Surely he can do something."

Ratchet nodded. Had he been a compassionate man, he might have felt sorry for Celia Wynd. Not being one, he just leaned back in his chair and smiled.

FOR A FEW moments after the ghost vanished, the children simply stared at one another.

"Well," said Edward, "I guess he told us off."

Jennifer was not impressed. "That was just bluster. I'll admit he wasn't the most cheerful ghost I've ever met."

"How many ghosts do you know?" asked Perry.

"Very funny. You know what I mean. It can't

be easy for him. He's sort of caught between two worlds."

"And he's probably a menace in both," said Alison, the dinner fiasco fresh in her mind.

"Even so," said Jennifer, "he needs our help."

Edward sighed. "Getting him to believe that will be difficult."

"True. The right plan will be complicated and devious."

In other words, it was perfect for the whole family.

"If he doesn't want our help," said Jamie, "maybe we shouldn't interfere."

"Where will that leave Aunt Celia?" said Edward.

"Without many dinner guests," said Alison.

"Or a house in good shape," added Perry.

"No question about it," said Jennifer. "We have to help this Henry Baldridge, whether he wants us to or not. So what if he's a bit stubborn? If I'd been a ghost for eighty-seven years, I'd be set in my ways, too."

"Look what you've done with only twelve," said Perry.

Jennifer wagged a finger at him. "Don't push your luck, Perry. I assume you want to reach your tenth birthday in one piece. There's not much room in here to dodge fireballs."

"All right, guys," said Alison, stepping between them, "Let's concentrate on the matter at hand. We have to put this wall back the way we found it."

"Then what?" asked Jamie.

"Then we tell Aunt Celia what's going on. She should have a say about what's done with a ghost in her own house." Alison sighed. "Let's hope she's strong enough to take the news."

THEY FOUND their aunt lying down with a cold compress across her forehead. Her eyes were closed.

"We should come back later," murmured Edward.

"You don't have to whisper," Aunt Celia said clearly. "I'm not asleep."

The children filed into the room.

"How are you feeling?" asked Jennifer.

"Weary, I'm afraid. Not tired, mind you, but weary. I just had another call from Mr. Ratchet."

"Aunt Celia, you're not letting him wear you down?"

"Not him, dear. But I can't help wondering if he has a point. I mean, look at the mess I've been making of things lately. Think of your shoes, the dinner with Grace ... My magic seems to have a mind of its own." She paused. "And twice now, I even thought I saw ... No, no, it's better not to discuss that."

"Aunt Celia," said Edward, "we have to talk to you. It has to do with the house ..."

"Which we love," noted Jennifer.

"Really," said Perry.

"A great place," Jamie put in.

Aunt Celia smiled. "I'm glad we have that settled. Was that all you wanted to tell me?"

Everyone looked to Alison. She sighed. There were times when being the oldest had its disadvantages.

"Not all," she said. "But because this is such a wonderful house ..."

"Are we going to start that again? Children, it's sweet of you to try and make me feel better ..."

"Sweet?" said Jamie.

"We're not being sweet," said Jennifer. "We know when we're being sweet, and this isn't it."

"True," said Edward, "we're just—"

"Your house is haunted," Perry declared.

The others stared at him.

"Well, you were taking all night," Perry said defensively.

Aunt Celia was staring the hardest of all. "Say that again," she said. "About the house, I mean."

"It's haunted," said Perry.

Aunt Celia was nodding. "What does that mean exactly?"

"You have a ghost living here," said Jennifer. If Perry could be direct, so could she.

"A ghost? A ghost!" Aunt Celia sat up and beamed. "An elderly fellow with white hair? Dressed like a butler or maybe a maitre d' in one of those fancy restaurants?"

"Why, yes," said Jamie. "Now don't be too upset. I'm sure—"

"Whoopee!" shouted Aunt Celia, jumping up from the bed.

"I think she's taking the news rather well," said Alison.

"Oh, children!" their aunt exclaimed. "What a relief!"

Jennifer frowned. "You're glad to find out a ghost lives here?"

"Of course. That means he exists, which is much better than thinking I was imagining him. I thought senility was setting in." She let out a deep breath.

"He's not a spooky ghost," Edward hastened

to add. "And he spoke most respectfully of you. There's no need for alarm."

"I'm not alarmed. Do I look alarmed? Of course, I don't. I'm delighted, that's what I am. I could've saved myself a lot of anguish by talking to him myself. But thinking he wasn't real, I didn't want to give my hallucination the satisfaction of knowing it had fooled me." She chuckled. "Having a ghost here should be interesting. Why, we might get to be friends."

"There is one other problem," said Alison. "The ghost is cursed."

This didn't faze Aunt Celia. "I expect a great many ghosts are. Poor fellow. Perhaps there's something we can do for him. Do you know what this curse is?"

"Not yet," Edward admitted.

"We will," she said confidently. "So when do I get to meet this ghost?"

"You'll have to find him first," muttered Perry.

"What's that, dear?"

"We didn't part on the best of terms," said Jamie.

"He's sort of shy," said Alison.

"I'll win him over," Aunt Celia said decisively.

The children weren't so sure, but they kept their opinions to themselves.

THE GHOST probably would have agreed with them. He was not feeling very sociable at present; he was feeling very confused. After leaving the children in his pantry, he had drifted down to the basement. The dusty brick and stone were not the pleasantest surroundings, but here at least he wouldn't be disturbed. What Henry needed most was time to think. He knew he had been impolite to the children, and this bothered him. As relatives of the master of the house, they were entitled to his respect. But their sudden arrival had been startling, as had been their ability to see and hear him.

"Most unusual, that was," he murmured.

He repeated this several times over the next few hours, but time means little to a ghost, and he was unaware of how long he had been sitting.

"Henry!"

This was not the voice of the children. As Henry turned, he found two other ghosts standing behind him. One was dressed in a seaman's garb; the other was wearing a blacksmith's heavy apron, and he had the brawny arms to go with it.

"We want to talk with you, Henry," the blacksmith said evenly. "Isn't that right, Mr. Briggs?" His voice rang out in precise strokes, like the sound of a hammer hitting an anvil.

"Absolutely, Mr. Hurley," the sailor noted. "It's been a long time, Henry."

"Many years," the older ghost conceded. His tone left little doubt that had many more years passed without their meeting, Henry would not have regretted it.

"Mr. Hurley," the sailor continued, "I do believe that Henry is not very fond of us."

"Come now," said Mr. Hurley, putting one arm around Henry's shoulder, "I'm sure you're imagining that." He squeezed Henry heartily in his stony fingers. "Isn't that right, Henry?"

Henry winced in his grip. One ghost was always vulnerable to the touch of another. "Mr. Briggs always did have an active imagination," he said.

The blacksmith released him. "You hear that, Mr. Briggs? A pretty compliment from the butler."

"Aye, I heard him." Mr. Briggs allowed himself a sly smile. "But on to the business at hand. We are here, Henry, on an errand for Ephraim Skags. You know Skags, I believe? Yes, I can see

that you do. Well, you haven't been as coopera-
tive with our plan as we expected, and now he
has need of this house so we expect your help."

"What? Why?"

"We're not here to answer your questions,
Henry. We're just messengers. Skags wants you
to encourage the old woman who lives here to
leave."

"But what has she—"

"Haunt her, Henry," said Mr. Hurley. "Turn
this house into her own personal nightmare."

"I won't" Henry said staunchly. "I serve the
master of this house, whoever it is."

"We're patient men," said the blacksmith.
"Aren't we, Mr. Briggs?"

"Without a doubt, Mr. Hurley. But even patient men have their limits. Henry, your new
master is an old woman, is she not?"

"Why, yes."

"A bit fragile, I suspect," said Mr. Briggs.
"Nerves not what they once were."

"I suppose so."

"Let us speak plainly," said Mr. Hurley.
"Should she leave at your bidding, she comes to
no harm. Should she leave at our bidding, it's
more difficult to say." He cracked his ghostly
knuckles.

"You wouldn't dare!"

"I'm not saying we'd enjoy it," Mr. Briggs said with a smile, "But I wouldn't go so far as to say we wouldn't dare. I've dared a great deal in my time. If you wish her to remain safe and well, you'll begin the haunting."

"But I—"

"Mr. Hurley, are you interested in excuses?"

"Not I, Mr. Briggs."

Henry bit his lip.

"We're in agreement, then," said the sailor. "Henry, we don't want excuses. We want results." He looked at Henry steadily. "Shall we go, Mr. Hurley?"

"At once, Mr. Briggs."

They strode through the wall laughing hollowly to themselves.

SEVEN

JENNIFER couldn't sleep. The room was comfortable enough, and so was the bed, but she remained wide awake. She had tried bunching her pillow, she tried smoothing it flat. She had lain on her left side, she had lain on her right. She had closed her eyes, she had opened them. She had counted sheep, she had counted the holes in the radiator cover. She had tried to think of a story, she had tried to think of nothing at all.

None of this had helped. She couldn't get the ghost off her mind.

When the clock downstairs struck one, Jennifer gave up. If she couldn't sleep, she might as well do something else. The wind whistling outside the window sent the shadows of branches snaking across her bedroom wall. The gently twisting tentacles gave Jennifer an idea.

On the moonlit wall, the shadowy outline of a proscenium stage appeared, a dark frame surrounding an open square. Into this box marched the silhouette of a clown with ruffled sleeves, huge shoes, and a pointed hat. With a twist of her fingers, Jennifer directed the clown's actions. He was an athletic fellow, twirling and somersaulting as fast as Jennifer could think of routines for him to perform. Some of his tumbles needed practice, but even his mishaps were fun to watch. So much fun, in fact, that Jennifer began to laugh at his antics.

She paused when the first wave of cold hit her. By now she knew what the feeling meant. She couldn't see the ghost, but that didn't prove anything. For all she knew, he was hiding in the walls. Was he watching her clown? He must be. She wanted to talk with him, but if she just spoke up, he'd probably pull another disappearing act. She needed a different approach.

Henry's eyes never left the stage. The sound of Jennifer laughing had drawn him upstairs. He felt dispirited after his conversation with the two ghosts. The shadow clown might not be able to help him, but it was a pleasant distraction from his troubles.

The clown was crouching now, looking

stealthily left and right. Then he threw back his arms in delight. Sweeping his arm from left to right, he beckoned to someone.

Henry turned around. Who was the clown looking at?

When he turned back, the clown had his hands on his hips and he was stamping his foot. He beckoned again.

Why, he's looking at me, Henry thought.

The clown was waiting.

Henry stepped into the room.

"Hello," Jennifer said softly.

The ghost froze.

"Please don't run off. We got started badly before. It doesn't have to be that way. We could be friends."

Henry's leg was halfway through the wall, but he pulled it back.

"Friends?" he said.

"That's right."

Nobody had wanted to be Henry's friend in almost a century. "I could use a friend now," he admitted. "But I haven't had one for a long time. I'm out of practice."

"It's like riding a bicycle," said Jennifer. "Once you learn, you never forget."

Henry sighed.

"What's the matter?"

"I never rode a bicycle. Didn't feel comfortable on such a contraption."

"Oh. Well, the bicycle itself isn't important. It's the idea that counts. If we're going to be friends, though, we should know each other's names. I know yours, Mr. Baldridge. Mine's Jennifer Wynd."

The ghost made a little bow.

"Call me, Henry, Miss Jennifer."

"I will if you'll drop the *Miss* stuff. Friends shouldn't be so formal."

"Oh, I couldn't, Miss Jennifer. It wouldn't be right."

"Why not?"

"A butler does not presume such familiarity with a member of his master's family."

"You're not our family butler. Aunt Celia never hired you."

"I know. I came with the house. A package deal you might say. The curse and the house come together."

Jennifer hesitated. "Could you tell me a little more about it?"

The ghost's expression softened. "It's swell of you to be so interested."

"Swell?"

"Nice, good, kind . . ."

Jennifer frowned. "I don't think people say *swell* anymore."

Henry looked embarrassed. "A pity. It was a fine word. Very expressive. But words come and go so quickly now. It's hard to keep up. Sometimes the fads pass so fast, they make my head spin."

"Really?" said Jennifer. "I saw a ghost do that in a movie once."

"Not *literally* spin," said Henry, drawing himself up to his full height. "It was a figure of speech. I may be a ghost, but I'm a dignified ghost."

"Sorry."

"Apology accepted. I will say it's nifty of you to want to help."

Jennifer nodded solemnly. Henry was still behind the times, but she didn't want to rub it in.

"Are all ghosts cursed?" she went on.

"Not all, but a large number. The others are usually tied to some personal tragedy." He frowned. "They don't have much to do with us. You see, they're ghosts by choice. We're not."

"Which brings us back to the curse . . ."

Henry took a deep breath. "I hesitate to speak ill of a former employer, but Mr. Dunstable's nature was certainly no secret. I knew him his whole life, and so had ample occasion to judge." Henry shuddered. "He was a most disagreeable child."

"Why did you put up with it?"

"I had worked for his parents for many years. When they died, I was no longer in my prime. I doubted that I could find a position elsewhere. Their will, however, provided me with a place in the household for as long as I should want it. Having no other prospects, I kept my place. Mr. Dunstable was tolerably satisfied with my performance at first, but as I got older, I became a trifle forgetful. Mr. Dunstable was a stickler for details, and details no longer were my strong point. When I began to forget whether he was home or not, he became furious."

"Was that really hard to keep track of?"

Henry smiled. "Being *at home* is a little more complicated than you might think. Oliver Dunstable was *at home* to the handful of visitors he wished to see. For the rest he was out."

"Just like that?" said Jennifer.

The ghost nodded.

"But that's so rude."

"The feelings of others did not interest Mr. Dunstable. There came a day when he had had enough. 'You have given me indigestion,' he said. 'You will do penance for that.' "

"The old grouch . . ." muttered Jennifer.

"He ranted at me for more than an hour. I took it stoically. Somehow that infuriated him even more. He would show me, he said. I would not take his curse so lightly. I did not believe he was serious, at least not until I died and found myself as you see me now."

"Could you end the curse?"

"Only by serving Mr. Dunstable in some important way, a way that would make up for my earlier indiscretions."

Jennifer frowned. "And you never managed that before he died? How awful. It left you doomed to be a ghost forever."

"Not necessarily. Over the years I have investigated the matter further. According to tradition, I cannot cancel the curse, but fulfilling its terms is still possible. You see, as Mr. Dunstable phrased the thing, if I served 'the master of the house in some crucially important way,' the curse would be lifted. Well, even after his passing, there continued to be masters of the house. I have tried to serve them in turn."

"But you're still here."

"Yes, I'm still here." Henry sighed. "The first

three new masters moved out of the house as soon as they learned it was haunted. The next three stayed, but they ignored my efforts to be of service. It's hard to serve a master who's ignoring you. In the beginning, I confined myself to a butler's regular duties. When that proved unsuccessful, I expanded my attempts. At this point, there are few areas of servitude that I have left unexplored. I've polished and dusted and cleaned my way through eighty-seven years without success. Your aunt is my seventh master. But judging by her reaction to me, she'll not be my last."

Jennifer considered for a moment. "Maybe you have to think bigger. I mean, even if you were the world's best shoe polisher, is a well-polished shoe really all that important? The world has changed since your day. Modern appliances must make it harder to help around the house. I don't know how fussy these curses are, but maybe you have to modernize your thinking. Have you tried following Aunt Celia around? Perhaps you could save her from being hit by a truck or something."

Henry shuddered. He thought about going outside—the traffic, the skyscrapers, the plastic raincoats.

"No."

"No?"

"I don't like going out," Henry stated flatly. "Those dangerous motor cars are everywhere."

"But they can't hit you, so why worry?"

"When a motor car is bearing down on you at great speed, you don't stop to consider that it will pass harmlessly through your body. I never had the strongest constitution . . . I'm easily startled."

"Look, the world is only going to get more and more startling over time. Do you want to buttle your way into the next millenium?"

The ghost winced at this prospect, but he had resigned himself to it. "I don't think your aunt can survive another attempt on my part to help her. After what happened at dinner . . ."

"Anyone can have a bad day," Jennifer insisted.

"I have had many bad days. I see what lies ahead. There is no fighting Fate, no arguing with Destiny."

"A few setbacks don't make you a failure. You can learn from your mistakes."

"I have. I've learned there's no use trying any further. I cannot bear any more disappointments. It will be simpler if I just accept what has happened and adjust as best I can."

Jennifer had a lot more to say, but before she

could continue, Jamie appeared in the doorway, yawning.

"Who are you talking to, Jen? Hey, it's the ghost!"

"Go away," Jennifer hissed. "You'll scare him. Henry and I are having a private little talk."

Jamie blinked. "Not anymore," he said.

He was right. The ghost was gone.

EIGHT

THE NEXT morning found the pale winter sunshine falling over a grumpy Jennifer Wynd. Things had been going so well the night before until Jamie had turned up. True, Henry had not been very cheery, but Jennifer thought she could have brought him around. As events now stood, Jennifer wasn't sure whether she and the ghost were even on speaking terms.

She was feeling no better when the others came in to hear the whole story.

"So the ghost has to do Aunt Celia a good deed, huh?" was how Perry summed up the situation.

"Not exactly," said Jennifer. "He has to serve her in some very important way."

"I gather the deed itself is now only part of

the problem" said Alison. "First we have to help Henry regain his confidence."

Jamie brightened. He was eager to redeem himself for having scared the ghost away. "I have an idea," he said. "Henry's down in the dumps because he thinks his situation's hopeless. He probably figures no ghost has ever been in the hole he's in and worked his way out of it. But what if he heard differently? What if he learned of other ghosts who didn't beat their curses at first, but won out in the end? I'll bet that would bring him around."

"It might," said Perry. "But where would he hear something like that?"

"From other ghosts?"

"Where will we find them?" said Jennifer.

"Right here," Jamie explained. "We'll be the ghosts."

"What about the stories?" asked Alison.

"We'll make them up."

The others laughed.

"Well, it may not be a brilliant plan," Jamie conceded, "but it's creative and resourceful. That should count for something."

"Not much," said Edward. "Won't Henry recognize us?"

"I doubt it. He's only talked to Jennifer for

any length of time, and that was in the dark. By the time we were done disguising—"

"How are you going to manage that?" asked Alison. "Henry's skin and his clothes are all the same color."

"And he glows," said Perry.

Jamie was not deterred. "We could whiten ourselves with flour. A glue spell would keep it on, and as for glowing, that would be easy."

"You want me to coat myself in flour?" said Alison. "What do you think I am, a fish filet?"

"Or fried chicken?" said Edward. "Nice try, Jamie, but forget it. We'll have to think of something else."

The appearance of Aunt Celia put to rest any further suggestions. The children had agreed not to tell her about this latest meeting with the ghost. She would want to help out, and Jennifer felt that Henry would be only further depressed at the prospect of his master trying to cheer him up.

Aunt Celia set breakfast in motion while the children set the table. She mixed the batter by hand, but once she poured out the pancakes, they flipped themselves on the griddle.

Perry was watching the pancakes closely. "How do they know when to turn?" he asked.

"Practice," said his aunt. "I was thirty before I could make pancakes without someone calling the fire department."

Other than Perry's comment, though, the children were unusually quiet. Aunt Celia noticed the silence, but she didn't dwell on it. Even vacationing children could be expected to have a few thoughtful moments.

"The weather looks uncertain today," she said, as they were clearing the table. "I suppose you hardy country souls won't mind that. Alison and Edward, don't forget, you promised to meet Miss Salisbury this morning."

They actually had forgotten. The last thing either of them wanted to do was go look at a lot of paintings; they had not been enthusiastic last night when they had found themselves planning the trip with Miss Salisbury. Now, with a glum ghost on the premises, they were even less eager. But they saw no way out of it.

Perry grinned. "You have to honor your commitments," he said sagely.

"I'm glad you feel that way," said his aunt. "As I recall, Perry, you have such a commitment with me."

"I do?"

"Carrying over from last year. We had a date with the Freedom Trail, one that was cancelled at the last minute."

"You remember, Perry," said Edward, "you developed that sudden cold."

"A convenient cold," Jennifer added. "But you're in the pink now."

Perry smiled weakly. "I'm not sure this is the time for a historical tour. Paul Revere's house can wait—"

"Nonsense," said Alison, "you've been culturally deprived for too long already. The Freedom Trail is a must. Just think, there's the State House, the Old North Church, a couple of graveyards—you'll have a great time."

Perry could see he was cornered.

"We'll leave directly," said Aunt Celia. She frowned. "Jamie, Jennifer, what will you do while we're gone?"

"Don't worry about us," said Jamie. "We'll be fine."

"We'll even clean up breakfast," said Jennifer. "That way the rest of you can get going."

"Goodness, I'm in shock," said the aunt. "You children must be turning over a new leaf."

Edward sent them a look. "Let's hope there's no trouble on the other side."

Jamie snorted. "Naturally we'll be model citizens."

Now it was Edward's turn to snort. Jamie and Jennifer were bound to look for Henry. The others didn't want to miss that, but with Aunt Celia ushering Edward and Alison into their coats and quizzing Perry on the history of Boston, they had no time to think about it further

"HOW DO I look?"

Jennifer laughed. "Like a dumpling. But a ghostly dumpling," she added, noting his disappointment.

"It's your turn," said Jamie.

Jennifer sighed. Now that the moment had come, she wasn't sure letting Jamie talk her into this had been such a good idea. He had been very persuasive, playing heavily on the "What harm can it do?" theme, and Jennifer had finally given in. They had gone out to buy two sacks of flour, and Jamie had used most of one on himself.

"Are you sure we're being model citizens?"

"What could be more model that helping out someone in distress?"

Jennifer thought back to Henry's plight.

When it came to distress, Henry certainly had more than his share.

"True," she said.

She emptied her sack onto the floor. The flour fell in a soft heap. Jennifer twirled her finger over its peak, and as she did, the flour began to rise. She directed the twister up one leg, then the other. When it reached her waist, she paused.

"What are you waiting for?" Jamie asked.

"Don't rush me."

Squeezing her eyes shut, she sucked in a huge breath, and raised the twister around her upper half. For a second she was enveloped in a white cloud, and Jamie could not see her clearly. When the cloud cleared, a chalky Jennifer stood before him.

"How do I look?" she asked, blinking.

He laughed.

"Oh, I look like you, huh?"

Jamie's laugh subsided. "I guess so. Now for the glue spell to make the flour stick."

"Glue spells always make me itchy," said Jennifer. "I suppose it can't be helped."

The spell was a short one. When it was done, Jennifer jumped up and down. The flour stayed put.

"The glow comes last," said Jamie. "Pointing a finger first at a lightbulb and then at himself, he was soon giving off a faint incandescence.

"Perfect," said Jennifer, doing the same thing.

"And the glow hides the color of our eyes, too. I think we'll pass."

Jennifer stared at her floury arm. "Let's just hope we don't end up in a frying pan . . ."

"Or a fire," said Jamie.

Knowing Henry's feelings about leaving the house, they were sure he was around somewhere. They found him at last in Perry's bedroom, trying to make the bed without any wrinkles in the blankets. Jamie and Jennifer stood in the doorway until he looked up.

"More messengers?" he said. "Has Skags taken to pressing children into his service?"

The Wynds did not understand this, but they went ahead with their plan.

"We have come to see you, Henry," said Jennifer, in as deep a voice as she could manage.

"You have become discouraged about your curse," Jamie declared darkly. "The Curse Committee has sent us—"

Henry frowned. "The Curse Committee? I've never heard of it."

Jamie ignored him. "The committee has followed your case closely. Your position is not the hopeless one you imagine it is. Your situation is not nearly as bad, for example, as was the lighthouse ghost who got lost in the fog."

Jennifer giggled. This was the first she had heard of the lighthouse ghost.

Jamie frowned at her.

"Sorry," she muttered, biting her lip. "You were saying . . ." She cleared her throat.

Henry looked at them more closely. "I know that laugh. Last night . . . Why, it's Miss Jennifer . . . And you . . . you're one of her brothers."

Jamie slumped disappointedly against the wall.

"What's the meaning of this masquerade?"

Jennifer sighed. "We were hoping to encourage you to keep fighting your curse."

"I thought I made my position quite clear," Henry said firmly. "I don't—"

"Why did you call us messengers from Skags?" asked Jamie, hoping to salvage the discussion.

"I was in error."

"We know you were in error. But who is this Skags?"

"Is he giving you trouble?" said Jennifer. "Is that why you can't concentrate on your curse?"

Henry shuddered. "I might as well tell you,"

he said. "If you're willing to go to these lengths"—he indicated the flour—"you'll only badger me until I spill the beans."

"Spill the beans?" said Jamie.

"Never mind," whispered Jennifer. "I'll explain later." She smiled at Henry. "Go on," she said.

"Skags won't like it, though," the ghost remarked.

"He doesn't have to know," said Jennifer. "It'll be our secret. Right, Jamie?"

"Right. Sealed lips and all that."

"Very well," said Henry. "I'll tell you what I know. A hundred years ago or more, Ephraim Skags worked at the Patriot Tavern. After his death, he haunted the place."

"Was he cursed, too?"

"Apparently, but how and why he never said. Whatever it was, the curse stood up. He's been a ghost longer than I have. But the Patriot Tavern was torn down last spring."

"I'll bet he was upset," said Jamie.

"Not Skags. Whatever his curse was, the destruction of the tavern freed him from staying there. It did not, however, free him from the curse. So he remains a ghost, but a ghost with no purpose assigned to him."

"Is that bad?" asked Jennifer.

Henry considered for a moment. "Not with some ghosts, perhaps. With a ghost like Skags, it's dangerous. He was bound to come into mischief sooner or later. It turned out to be sooner."

"But how does that involve you?" asked Jamie.

"Because Skags's mischief concerns other ghosts. He wants us to organize. He thinks we should assert ourselves." Henry paused. "Hundreds of ghosts working together could cause a lot of trouble. And with Skags as their leader . . ." Henry shook his head.

"Well," said Jennifer, "you won't have to fight him alone."

"I don't plan to fight him. I don't approve of his plans, but I am hardly one to lead the opposition. A butler makes less than an inspiring figure."

"I would follow you," Jennifer said staunchly.

"I appreciate that," Henry conceded. "But in any event it would be unwise for you to become involved. You would only get hurt. Skags doesn't take kindly to anyone meddling in his affairs. Besides . . ."

"We don't have to help as people," interrupted Jamie. "We can help as ghosts."

Henry looked skeptical. "I admit you fooled

me briefly. But whether you would fool an intelligent ghost for long enough to—" He suddenly stiffened.

Jennifer shivered.

"What's the matter, Jen? Is . . ." Jamie never finished his question. The sight of the ghostly blacksmith standing to his left answered it for him.

"Little ghosts," Mr. Hurley stated.

If he was looking for an argument, he didn't get one.

"That's right," said Jennifer. "Little ghosts. Anything wrong with that, Buster?"

The blacksmith frowned. "My name is not Buster." He turned to Henry. "Skags wants to see you. Now."

"May we come, too?" asked Jamie.

"My orders are only for the butler." Mr. Hurley wished Mr. Briggs had come along. Mr. Briggs always knew what to do in unexpected situations.

"The little ghosts may follow," he decided. "Many ghosts will be there. Two more cannot matter. Come, Henry."

Taking the butler's arm, he ushered him down the stairs and through the living room wall.

Jamie and Jennifer stared at each other.

"If we don't want to lose them," said Jennifer, "we'd better hurry."

"Like this?" said Jamie.

Jennifer didn't answer. She simply ran out the front door.

NINE

A BITTER WIND was blowing down Chestnut Street. Henry didn't feel it; he never felt the weather. In pouring rains, when people turned into soggy lumps, Henry was bone dry. On humid afternoons, when starchy collars wilted in the sun, not one bead of sweat crossed Henry's brow. And on this, a brisk December day, even though he was without a coat, hat, scarf, or gloves, he was perfectly comfortable.

Jamie and Jennifer could not say the same. Their magical glow protected them from the worst of the cold, but it was no substitute for a winter coat.

"Can we generate more heat?" Jamie wondered.

"It might melt the glue spell."

"Let's risk it."

"Let's not. As long as we're here, we're not going to take any chances."

"But I'm cold."

"If you need to take your mind off the weather, look at the attention we're getting."

Jamie had been concentrating on staying warm. Now he looked around.

"People are staring," he whispered.

"I know. I have eyes."

"What should we do?"

"Ignore them," said Jennifer. "This is the big city. People see weirdos here all the time."

"I don't like being one of them."

"The flour *was* your idea," she reminded him.

Jamie kept quite after that.

They would have liked to ask Henry where they were going, but he and the blacksmith were several yards ahead of them, and neither looked in the mood for conversation. The blacksmith set a fast pace, and the children had to skip along to match his strides.

"This place looks familiar..." said Jamie. "That's where Edward took our picture. Or at least that's where he was supposed to. Instead he—"

"Look!" cried Jennifer.

What she saw, Jamie saw, too. Several ghosts were walking through the fence that surrounded the Patriot Center construction site. Henry glanced back to check on the Wynds' progress just before he was pulled through by the single-minded blacksmith.

The children approached the fence.

"We can't fake this," Jamie muttered.

Jennifer was loosening one of the boards. "True, but with a little magical boost, we can squeeze through." Her spell pried back the wood, and she ducked through the hole.

Jamie was right behind her.

Beyond the fence was a giant concrete hole, the foundation for a skyscraper that was still just a gridwork of steel girders. A giant crane stood poised over it, and two bulldozers were sitting on either side. Jamie and Jennifer paid them little attention. They were staring instead at the few dozen ghosts who were gathered around them.

"Wouldn't it have been easier to walk through the fence?" asked a ghost on their left.

"Are you speaking to me?" Jennifer asked.

The ghost nodded. "You climbed through a hole in the fence. Why go to all that trouble? Why not just walk through?"

"We're pretending to be real children," said Jennifer. "It's a game."

"I see." The ghost turned to his companion. "What a pity," he whispered. "Who would ever put a curse on a child?"

"I don't know, but it must have been a truly terrible curse. Even for ghosts, they're very pale."

The ghost on Jamie's right was staring at him. "You're very young for a ghost," she said.

"I know that," he replied.

"Particularly young for a curse," the ghost went on.

"Sad, isn't it?"

The ghost agreed. "I'd be interested to hear what happened."

"You would?"

"Certainly."

"You wouldn't be bored?"

"Not at all."

"Oh." Jamie took a deep breath. "It was my sister who did it. You know the kind. All sweetness and light to adults, but she kicks you under the table when no one is looking."

The ghost looked thoughtful. "I had a sister once. It was long ago."

"I'll bet, but you don't forget things like that.

Well, my sister used to curse me regularly. Of course, I didn't think much of it . . ." Jamie looked down at his floury stomach. "Who knew she had the power to do something like this?"

"Who, indeed?" said the ghost.

Jamie was warming up to his subject. "Of course, it wouldn't have mattered had I been paying more attention that day at the beach. But I wasn't expecting that cliff to be there, and . . ."

He shook his head sadly.

"Ah," said the ghost, "and that left your sister's latest curse hanging over you."

"It was fresh that morning. She had accused me of using her toys without asking."

"Had you?"

"Naturally. What else are they good for?"

"This curse, do you know how to break it?"

Jamie didn't.

"Tragic," said the ghost. "You have my sympathy."

That was more than Jennifer was giving him. She thought he had been pouring it on a little thick. Fortunately, she shut up as one of the ghosts stepped out onto a girder and turned to address them. Jennifer grimaced. Even at that distance, the ghost's appearance was very unpleasant. His face seemed frozen into a permanent snarl, and his bulky body moved with a menacing strength.

The ghosts fell silent to listen.

"I welcome you here today. You are here at my bidding, but not to serve me. You are here to serve yourself."

The ghosts murmured their approval. This was the kind of speech they liked to hear.

"Some of you," the speaker went on, "have been ghosts a long time."

"I came over on the *Mayflower*," said one fellow in the back.

"I was at Valley Forge," shouted another.

The speaker nodded. "I claim no fancy heritage. Most of you know me. I am Ephraim Skags. More than a century ago I worked at recruiting"—he smiled cruelly—"sailors for the long voyages to China. The Patriot Tavern was my base. The owner and I were partners. But when he died, his wife took over the property. She didn't approve of my, ah, recruitment practices. So she shut down the business and gave me a job at the bar. But by then I had my expenses to consider and appearances to keep up. One day we had a disagreement over the distribution of profits. She accused me of cheating her. Me!" He laughed. "Imagine that!" His laughter faded. "I cared nothing for her rantings and ravings, but she was not finished. She cursed me to spend a hundred years in that blasted tavern. Keeping track of receipts, she said." One of his fists clenched involuntarily. "Seventy-three years have come and gone since I began serving my term. As you can see, though,"—he gestured broadly—"the tavern is no more. Two months ago, it was torn down to make room for this new skyscraper. And without the tavern here, I find myself free to wander abroad."

Skags grinned—not prettily, but he got the job done. "How many of you feel that you were justly cursed?" he asked.

"Never!"

"I was framed!"

"Double-crossed!"

"Betrayed!"

Skags motioned for silence. "I thought so. Like myself, you all have wrongs that need righting. The time for that has come."

The ghosts gave him their full attention.

"Those who cursed us have long since passed outside our grasp, leaving us to deal with a world that grows more and more uncomfortable. But it need not be this way. What if you could choose your own environment? What if you could recreate at least a small piece of the world you knew?"

"A pleasant prospect," said a ghost in a waist-coat and knee-breeches, "but we would need money and power to do such things."

Skags nodded. "Let me explain further. You all know ghosts who haunt houses, but their motives extend no further than anger or love or petty frustrations. What a waste! If we want money and power, all we need do is make a business of haunting."

A surprised murmur passed through the crowd.

"Would such a thing work?" asked the ghost next to Jamie.

"It already has—on a small scale. My great-great grandson, Horace Ratchet, is a real estate agent, and we have become partners. Our operation is very straightforward. He decides which properties should be bought. I haunt them. Soon the owners wish to sell, and at bargain prices. Young Ratchet snaps them up, the hauntings stop, the properties regain their previous value, and we go on from there. Imagine, though, what we could accomplish if we were all haunting buildings at once."

The sun went behind a cloud. The ghosts were stirred, and not by the wind, which was picking up as the sky darkened. It was an interesting plan.

"He sounds serious," said Jennifer.

"Deadly serious," Jamie agreed. "We're going to have to stop him."

Some of the ghosts were skeptical that people could be so easily scared. Surely the thing could not be accomplished as simply as Skags explained it.

He had expected this. "I did not come here to convince you with words alone. I have arranged a demonstration for this evening. I am going to put one of the fanciest hotels in the city out of business. If you will gather at the northeast corner of the Public Garden at midnight, I will show you what a little haunting can do."

The ghosts stood up and prepared to leave.

"We should go," said Jamie. He eyed the sky warily. "It looks like rain."

"Not without Henry," Jennifer insisted. "I don't like the way that blacksmith is holding him."

While most of the ghosts were drifting away, Mr. Hurley and Mr. Briggs were ushering Henry up to Skags himself. The speaker did not look pleased. He glared at the butler for a full minute.

"I'm very disappointed in you, Henry," he said finally. "My associates tell me you are not enthusiastic about helping me out."

"It does not fall within the realm of my regular duties."

Skags tapped his chin. "That's quite true." He turned to Mr. Briggs. "You warned him what will happen?"

"We warned him. He's risking the old woman getting a terrible fright."

"Well, Henry," said Skags, "the choice is—"

"You big bully!" said Jamie, rushing forward.

"Leave him alone!" Jennifer shouted.

Skags looked at the children in surprise. "What's this?" he said. "I didn't know you had friends, Henry."

"They're young, Skags," sputtered the butler. "Pay them no mind."

"We're not leaving without you, Henry," Jamie declared.

"Well, well," said Skags. "Very good friends, it seems."

While he considered this new development, the rain began to fall. It made no difference to the three actual ghosts, but Jamie and Jennifer were not so unaffected. The rain was dissolving the glue spell, causing the flour underneath to dribble down their faces and clothes.

Skags eyed them sharply.

"Why, they're not ghosts at all," he snapped. "It's a disguise. What's going on here, Baldridge?"

Henry assumed a more formal air. "Allow me to introduce Jamie and Jennifer Wynd."

"Wynd? Related to Miss Celia Wynd, no doubt."

"What of it?" said Jennifer. "She's our great-aunt."

"You're a spunky lot." Skags frowned. "But how is it they can see and hear us. Surely they're not blood relations."

"I don't know how they manage that," Henry admitted, "but obviously they do. They're harmless, though. You needn't bother with them."

"On the contrary, I always bother with spies. Besides, Henry, I note that you seem to care for them. Therefore they will remain with me while you carry out your appointed task."

He threw back his head and laughed.

"I think it's time to go," said Jamie.

Jennifer agreed.

Mr. Briggs barred their way. "You heard what Skags said. You're not going anywhere."

"We'll see about that." Jennifer held out her hand, and a fireball the size of an orange appeared. It blazed brightly despite the rain.

"Now you step aside, or I'll have to use this."

"Do you see that, Mr. Hurley?"

"I certainly do, Mr. Briggs."

Skags had seen it, too. "The girl is full of stupid tricks," he said.

"Last chance to move," said Jennifer.

Mr. Briggs stood his ground.

"Don't say I didn't warn you." She threw the fireball at the waiting sailor. It went right through him, sputtering harmlessly against a girder.

"Oh-oh," she said.

Mr. Hurley rushed forward and grabbed the children roughly by the arm. "No more tricks," he said. "I don't like tricks."

"You see," said Mr. Briggs, "we can alter our state at will. When threatened"—he paused as Jennifer tried to kick him—"we simply dematerialize."

Jennifer's foot went right through him. She lost her balance and fell down.

Skags nodded. "Remember what I said,

Henry. If you don't start haunting that Wynd woman at once, not only will she suffer, but these young friends of yours will meet with an unfortunate accident. Now, go!"

Henry went.

TEN

"THERE MUST have been a mistake," said Edward.

Alison closed the door behind him.

"So you're not the world's greatest photographer. Don't worry about it."

"I'm telling you these aren't the pictures I took. I saw those pale guys walk through the wall."

"Let me look again." She flipped through the snapshots. "These are yours, all right. Actually, I think you did a good job. The words Patriot Center are nice and sharp."

"Ha, ha."

Alison took off her coat. "Anyway, you can worry about it another time. We've got to tackle that ghost now. Hello!" she called out. "Jamie? Jennifer? We're back!"

Her greeting rang through the house without snaring a reply.

"Anybody home?" shouted Edward.

The silence continued.

"I guess not," he said. He glanced at his watch. "We were out longer than I thought. It's four o'clock. I'm hungry."

"How can you be hungry? Miss Salisbury treated us to those crepes only an hour ago."

"I'll bet no one has ever filled up on crepes," said Edward. "They're just decorations for your stomach. Let's see what's in the refrigerator."

The sight of the kitchen, however, put all thoughts of eating out of their heads.

"Look at this!" exclaimed Alison. "Flour everywhere! What a mess. If they decided to bake, why didn't they clean up afterward?"

Edward frowned. "I'm not sure they were baking at all. Remember the idea Jamie had this morning? What if he went ahead and tried it."

"Jennifer would never let him do that."

Edward glanced around. "There are two empty bags of flour," he noted.

Alison shook her head. "I should have said Jennifer would never let Jamie try it alone."

"Well, we'd better clean the place up before

Aunt Celia gets home. Imagine what she'd say if she knew."

They began wiping down the counters and floor.

"Edward," Alison said thoughtfully, "Jamie's plan was dumb, wasn't it?"

"Very."

"Well, if they tried it, and it didn't work, why aren't they here now?"

Edward hadn't considered this. "After we finish in here, let's find Henry and ask him."

They started with the basement and worked their way up. There was no sign of the ghost until they reached Perry's bedroom. "He was here, all right. Perry makes his bed only under a threat of death."

"What would make him stop in the middle?" wondered Edward.

"Maybe the sight of two floury children."

"Maybe. But why wouldn't he finish the bed afterward? You know, once he had exposed them. I mean, where would they go? Jennifer said Henry hates to go out."

They heard the door shut down below. There were footsteps on the stairs.

"Jamie? Jennifer? Is that you?" said Alison.

"No, it's me," said Perry, appearing in the

doorway. He looked from his brother and sister to his half-made bed. "Are you two practicing?" he asked. "Feel free to make my bed whenever you want."

"Thanks, but no thanks," said Edward. "We're looking for Jamie and Jennifer. We think they were up here with Henry."

"We also think they gave Jamie's plan a try," said Alison.

"Really?" said Perry. "And you say they're not here now. That's a bad sign."

"How do you mean?" asked Edward.

"They may be having all the fun by themselves."

"That's the least of our concerns," said Alison. She paused. "Where's Aunt Celia?"

"In the living room. She's checking on how many children Paul Revere had. She kept losing track at eight."

Edward looked out the window. "It's dark already. We'll have to tell her what's going on."

A sudden burst of laughter from below made them jump.

"Who was that?" asked Alison.

"Aunt Celia, I think," said Edward.

They rushed downstairs, pulling up short in the living room doorway. Henry and Aunt Celia were standing before them.

"Boo!" said the ghost.

Aunt Celia smiled at him. "They told me all about you, but they didn't say how funny you were. 'Boo!' I love it!"

Henry wasn't loving it. He raised his arms and tried to look fierce. "Boooooooooo!" he cried.

Aunt Celia started to laugh. And once she had started, she found it difficult to stop.

Henry's arms dropped to his sides. There was a limit to the humiliation he could endure. It was bad enough to have to behave in such an embarrassing manner. But not to be taken seriously while doing so . . .

"What's going on?" Edward demanded.

Henry sighed. "I tried," he said. "Nobody can say I didn't."

"Tried what?"

"Haunting your aunt. But I have no aptitude for it. Not that I'm surprised, mind you."

"Why would you want to haunt Aunt Celia?" asked Alison.

He explained what had happened at the construction site.

The news sobered Aunt Celia quickly. "I don't know this Ephraim Skags," she said, "but his story rings true. The Patriot Tavern was once infamous for shanghaiing sailors; though Skags, of course, wouldn't call it that. Florence

Murphy was the widow who cleaned up that racket. I presented a paper on her once to the historical society. A fascinating woman in her later years . . ."

"What's our next move?" said Perry.

"We must rescue them," said Aunt Celia. "And we would do well to teach Skags and Mr. Ratchet a lesson, too."

"Henry, all this happened hours ago," said Alison. "Where have you been since then?"

"Wandering around. I was most distraught."

"But I thought you hated the outdoors."

The ghost reflected on this. "That only shows you how upset I was."

"Enough time has been wasted," said Edward. "You must lead us back to them at once."

Henry shook his head. "I could never follow Mr. Hurley's path. I wasn't paying any attention. I only found my way back here by accident. The city had changed greatly since last I ventured out."

"Then what are we going to do?"

Henry paced the room. He couldn't help feeling responsible for the current predicament, and it made him jumpy. As he fretted, his eye fell on the discarded pictures Edward had placed on the table.

"Oh!" he said.

"What is it, Henry?" asked Alison.

The ghost picked up the pictures. "This is where we went. I remember the sign. It was this Patriot Center."

Aunt Celia blinked. "Of course! What more appropriate place could Skags pick for his little meetings?"

"You can take us there, can't you?" said Perry.

"I should say so. It's on Canal Street. Or is it Wharf Avenue? Well, I'll know it when I see it."

"I was right, after all," said Edward, looking at the pictures again. "It's too bad the ghosts didn't photograph well."

Aunt Celia stood up. "Maybe it wasn't their good side. Come, children, in these situations, there's no time to waste." She paused. "This is one of *those* situations, isn't it?"

They nodded.

Aunt Celia sighed. "That's what I thought."

IN THE OFFICES of Ratchet Real Estate, the president of the firm was rubbing his hands together.

"So, tonight's the big night, eh?" he said. Ratchet was pleased. Once the other ghosts had seen the demonstration, they would be only too eager to join the cause. And with dozens of ghosts out doing his bidding, he would soon break ground for that skyscraper with his name on it. He could already imagine the prominent place it would occupy on the skyline.

"Yes, tonight it is," said Skags. "We should have no problems now that the children are out of the way."

"Children?"

Skags filled him in.

"I don't like it," said Ratchet. "I mean, holding children prisoner . . ."

"Bah!" muttered Skags. "Don't go soft on me now. Remember, you have my blood running through your veins."

Ratcher swallowed hard. "I know, but children . . ."

"We cannot afford to take chances. I will only get one opportunity to convince the other ghosts to join us. They will not easily change their ways. That's why the demonstration is so important. When these children popped up from nowhere, what was I supposed to do? Coddle them?"

Ratchet mopped his brow with a handkerchief. He didn't like it when Skags stared at him like that.

"Where are they now?"

"Briggs and Hurley have them hidden away." Skags shook his head. "That girl's a lot of trouble, maybe more trouble than she's worth."

Ratchet got up and began pacing the room. "You wouldn't resort to violence?" he asked.

Skags spat. "You haven't objected to it so far, not when it's put so much money in your pocket."

Ratchet ran a hand over the top of his head. "Things have been profitable now, I admit. But, well, scaring people out of buildings is one thing . . ."

Skags snorted. "Stop sniveling! Don't make me sorry I involved you in my plans. Great-great grandson or not, if you crumble on me, you'll pay dearly for it."

Ratchet swallowed hard. He thought again of the Ratchet Building. "All right, all right, do what you like with the children." He hesitated. "What will you *do* with them?"

Skags laughed. "Whatever is necessary," he said.

THE WYNDS descended on the construction site like avenging angels prepared to do battle. Unfortunately there was no battle to be had. The place was deserted. They each took turns calling to Jamie and Jennifer, but their calls went unanswered.

"Maybe they left a clue showing where they've gone," said Perry.

"I don't even see clues proving they were here," said Edward.

"We could go out looking . . ." said Perry.

"Where would we start?" said Alison. "This isn't Westbridge. They could be anywhere."

Aunt Celia stared at a puddle. "I'm afraid that's true," she said.

With the trail at a dead end, they returned home in soggy spirits. The rain turned to snow as the temperature had dropped, but nobody was cheered by the flakes swirling around them.

Henry was waiting for them in the hall.

"Did you find them?" he asked anxiously.

Their faces answered the question for him.

"We'll have to wait till midnight," said Alison. "You're sure about the time and place, Henry?"

"Oh, yes. The northeast corner of the Public Garden, Skags said."

There was nothing to do but wait. Nobody felt much like talking, and the silence held until the phone rang at eleven o'clock.

Aunt Celia answered it.

"Hello? Yes, hello, Grace? What's that? Oh, you've been out walking, tonight. Grace I'm not sure this is the time to . . . True, Grace, you do sometimes see strange sights in the city. You saw one tonight. Well, you were probably due . . . Say that again . . . Are you sure, Grace? Two children covered in white paste."

Edward, Alison, and Perry sat up.

"Yes, yes," said Aunt Celia. "I can well imagine Hector barking at them. Barking and cowering at once . . . That does sound unusual. He wanted to follow them . . . I would have been glad to have a leash, too . . . No, Grace, I don't know what got into him. Oh, there's more . . . You thought the children looked like Jamie and Jennifer? My, that is a coincidence. Yes, it certainly is a small world . . . I know you would never even think of asking if Jamie and Jennifer are with me. That's a comfort, Grace, it truly is. Oh, the children are calling to me. I have to go. I'll talk to you tomorrow. 'Bye."

She hung up the phone.

The children had their coats on already.

ELEVEN

THE ARRIVAL of the ghosts in the Public Garden was not marked with any fanfare. They arrived singly or in small groups, gathering in a flowerbed at one edge of the drained lake. There were few passersby at that hour, and they hurried by in the deepening gloom, unaware of the ghosts in their midsts.

One group of onlookers, though, was studying the ghosts' every move. The Wynds had taken up a crouching position behind the parapet on the footbridge. Henry was with them, having taken Jennifer's advice to heart. With all that was likely to happen, he might never have a better chance to serve Aunt Celia.

"I hate this waiting," said Edward.

"So do I," said Alison.

"Me, too," Perry chimed in. He yawned. "How long has it been?"

Edward consulted his watch. "Almost an hour."

"The time is coming," Aunt Celia observed. "I can feel it."

"Does the waiting bother you, Henry?" Perry asked.

The ghost butler shrugged. "I have grown accustomed to it. I can remember dinner parties that seemed to go on for days."

All the ghosts seemed to have Henry's patience. With the time they had at their disposal, a few minutes of waiting were of little importance. They talked quietly among themselves, but made no other moves.

"Let's get them now!" hissed Perry.

"Not yet, dear," cautioned Aunt Celia. "We should hold off for a bit. We don't want to scare the ghosts away before Jamie and Jennifer arrive. We might never find them again."

From a tactical standpoint, Aunt Celia may have been right, but that didn't make Perry squirm any less.

"I see them!" hissed Alison.

Jamie and Jennifer were approaching the other ghosts in the unceremonious grip of Mr. Hurley and Mr. Briggs respectively. Their glows were intact, but the flour had streaked and fallen into messy clumps that dotted their faces and clothes. Neither of them looked happy.

"Jennifer sure looks mad," Edward noted.

Perry had seen this look directed at him many times. "Are you sure we have to rescue her?"

The others glared at him.

All right, all right, I was just asking."

"They look unharmed," said Aunt Celia. "Their pride, perhaps, is a little dented. Not to worry, though. Those dents have a wonderful way of hammering themselves out."

"Should we move in?" asked Edward.

Henry cleared his throat. "If I might make a suggestion? It would be best to wait until Skags declares himself."

"He's right," said Alison. "We have to do more than rescue Jamie and Jennifer. We have to stop Skags's scheme."

Perry huddled in his coat. "How are we going to manage that?"

"I wish I knew."

THE CLOCK in the church beyond the Common began to strike. Midnight had arrived.

The blacksmith and the sailor exchanged glances.

"Mr. Hurley, I believe it's time."

"You're right, Mr. Briggs. The hour has come."

They put Jamie and Jennifer into the keeping of some other ghosts and strode toward the front of the group.

"That's better," said Jamie. "We may be surrounded, but at least we're not being held. Boy, that blacksmith has some grip."

"I'm just glad we're out of that basement."

Jamie nodded. "It was dark and smelly. I thought something had died in there. It wasn't easy resisting the urge to escape."

"Well, it's good we did. It would't help things if we escaped. We have to stop this Skags guy. And what better way to keep an eye on him than by staying his prisoner?"

"I wish our magic worked better on these ghosts, though. The spells don't seem to do much. Did you see me trying to make Mr. Hurley fall asleep? He kept waving his arms, as if a mosquito were buzzing him, but he didn't actually get tired. The most I made him do was blink. Maybe with more time—"

Jamie stopped because Mr. Briggs was calling for the ghosts' attention.

"You were promised a demonstration," he said. "Even as I speak, Mr. Skags is in the Garden Hotel across the street. He is waking the guests in his own unique way—a way they will never forget. These guests won't sleep again this night. And when word spreads, the hotel will be ruined. Prospective buyers of the property will find themselves accompanied by one of us as they tour the premises. Naturally what they see and feel will discourage them from making an offer. This will clear the way for our agent to acquire the building at a bargain price. The plan is foolproof. Nothing can stop us."

Sudden shouts came from the hotel. Apparently Skags was making progress.

A man rushed out to a balcony in his pajamas.

"Ghosts! Ghosts!" he cried.

The ghosts below smiled at one another. This promised to be very entertaining.

Not to Jennifer. This was her big chance. She flicked her hand at the frightened man. He went on yelling, but no sound came from his mouth.

"That's one," Jamie whispered, "but you can't stop Skags that way. Even if we shut the guests up for now, they're bound to ruin the hotel's reputation later on. After all, we can't shut them up forever."

"If we can't stop them, who can?"

Jamie smiled. "It's just possible they'll stop

themselves. They won't report anything if they think they imagined it. What we have to do is make them think they're dreaming."

"They'll have to see some pretty strange things to make them think that."

Jamie bent down and began making snowballs.

"What are you doing?" Jennifer asked.

"You've heard of fireworks. How about snow-works? That will be plenty strange for starters."

As the other balconies filled with distraught guests, their voices were suddenly stilled. Jamie was throwing the snowballs up into the air, and Jennifer was adding a magical boost that sent them high overhead. At the height of each toss, the snowball exploded in a shower of colorful crystals that drifted toward the hotel.

Their rescuers watched this new development with interest.

"Look!" said Alison. "They're creating a diversion! Now they can escape."

"That's no diversion," said Aunt Celia. "It's something else."

"They're not trying to escape," said Perry. "They're trying to mess up Skags. We should be helping them. Why should they have all the fun?"

"If Skags succeeds in ruining the reputation of the hotel," said Henry, "the ghosts will do his bidding. He'll rouse everyone in the building. The bad publicity will do the rest."

"Alison," said Edward, "can we put a sleeping spell over the guests on the upper floors?"

"Maybe. But that won't help the ones Skags has already gotten to."

"That's all right. I'm not sure what Jamie and Jennifer are up to, but they seem to have a plan. We'll be busy enough as it is."

More and more guests were rushing out to their balconies, but the shouts framed in their minds died on their lips. Were those two trees really dancing a waltz across Charles Street? As for that lamppost doing cartwheels . . .

"That last drink really packed a whollop!"

"My nightmares aren't usually in color."

"Indigestion.. It's all indigestion."

Sheepishly, the guests returned inside, shaking their heads over their imaginations.

When Skags emerged from the hotel, he looked very pleased with himself. He was slightly troubled that he hadn't been able to awaken any guests on the top two floors, but the others would be enough to accomplish his purpose. Forcing them out onto their balconies had been an especially good touch. They would attract more attention that way. He could already see the headlines in the next day's papers . . .

As he crossed the street, he looked up, expecting the side of the hotel to be enveloped in bedlam. Instead, he saw the last of the guests sleepily returning to their rooms. Skags just stood and stared. A car passed right through him. He didn't even flinch.

Skags didn't know what had gone wrong, but a quick glance at Jamie and Jennifer convinced him that they were involved. The way that girl was moving her arms . . .

Henry had managed to worm his way into the middle of the increasingly restless ghosts. They had been expecting a good show, and they were sorely disappointed. If this was Skags's idea of brilliant planning, he and his schemes were as foolish as they looked. Henry watched their faces, waiting for just the right moment.

"You're a fake, Skags!" he shouted at last. Then he ducked out of sight.

Skags searched angrily for the owner of that voice, but it was too late. The damage had been done.

"Why are we wasting our time here?" asked one ghost.

"I've got better things to do."

"Who doesn't?"

"I've almost got my curse solved."

"Me, too."

The ghosts started to leave.

"Come back! Come back!" Skags ordered them. "Don't leave now. I can fix everything."

The ghosts weren't interested.

"Funny, Skags, very funny."

"Next time you plan a performance, make sure you've had enough rehearsals."

Skags clenched his fists. They might all be cowards and fools, but he was not ready to give up yet. That hotel was still his for the asking.

"Briggs! Hurley! Come with me!"

The blacksmith and the sailor remained where they were. Skags had promised them a foolproof plan. Instead they were smarting under the pitying glances of the other ghosts.

"What do you say, Mr. Briggs?" asked the blacksmith.

"I'll tell you, Mr. Hurley. I'm reminded of something my captain once told me as we were rounding the Horn. 'Briggs,' he said, 'it's time to leave a sinking ship when the water is lapping at your feet.' "

"I take your meaning," said Mr. Hurley. He shrugged mightily, and the two of them walked off together.

"Turncoats! Traitors!" cried Skags.

Nobody was listening to him. The ghosts were streaming away. It was then that the Wynds stood up.

"Perfect," said Edward.

They were ready to move in. They had not reckoned, however, with the path the retreating ghosts might take. Many of them were coming right over the bridge. The Wynds froze. They were not afraid of the ghosts, but that didn't mean they could bring themselves to charge right through them.

When the last ghost had passed, the Wynds pressed forward.

Jamie was picking himself up from the ground. He was covered with snow.

"What happened?" asked Alison.

"Skags rushed over. I tried to stop him." He rubbed his shoulder. "I didn't."

"Where's Jennifer?"

"Skags took her with him."

Everyone glanced around quickly. Jennifer was nowhere in sight.

TWELVE

THE SNOW was falling harder, but nobody seemed to notice.

"We must find her soon," said Henry. "Skags is in a bitter mood."

"Where would they go?" asked Alison.

"Look!" said Perry, pointing up Beacon Street. A glowing trail of footprints studded the snow. "Jennifer left those. I'd know those big feet anywhere."

"And where she goes," said Jamie, "we will follow."

Aunt Celia waved them on. "Don't wait for me," she told them. "Henry and I will catch up with you."

The Wynds dashed away up Beacon Hill. It was a long run through the city streets, but they kept a good pace, even after their sides began to ache. The trail was easy to follow. It took a straight line without any false turns. Wherever Skags was going, his mind was clearly made up about it.

The footprints led at last to the Patriot Center construction site. The sign had been roughly kicked in, and the Wynds ducked through the hole into the darkness beyond.

Edward blinked at the snow-covered mounds of dirt and debris. "They could be anywhere," he murmured.

"Not anywhere," said Jamie. "Look!"

He pointed up. Skags was climbing a ladder up the skeleton of the building, pulling Jennifer behind him. She was kicking him in the shins, and for once she was connecting with his ghostly legs. Unfortunately Skags was ignoring her blows.

"Let her go!" Alison shouted.

"That's right, you big ape!" said Jennifer. "Let me go."

"Oh, really?" Skags snapped, his eyes glittering. He pulled Jennifer onto a girder that stretched out like the plank of a pirate ship. "I could oblige you, of course."

"Could we float her down?" Edward whispered.

Alison shook her head. "She's too high. She'd fall too fast, and we couldn't control where she'd land."

"Skags!" shouted Edward. "You might as well release her. Your plans are ruined. You gain nothing this way."

Skags laughed, a high, eerie cry that echoed off the silent buildings around them. "Nothing?" he cried. "Hardly that. I will gain revenge. As you say, my plans are spoiled. Somehow I think losing this girl will spoil yours." He yanked her toward the girder's edge.

Edward stepped forward.

"Come any closer," Skags growled, "and she falls into the pit."

"He means it," said Jamie. "What are we going to do?"

They didn't know.

"We have to distract Skags," said Alison, "long enough to get Jennifer away somehow."

Jamie tapped her on the shoulder and pointed toward the crane.

It's not close enough," she murmured.

"Couldn't we swing the cable?"

Alison hadn't thought of that. "If we all pitch in . . ."

Edward nodded. "We'll have to time it just right. Perry, get Skags's attention and hold it."

Perry walked out of the gloom and onto a pile of crushed bricks, all that was left of the once bustling tavern. "Listen, you big windbag!" he shouted. "Let go of my sister or I'll turn you into . . . into . . . whatever ghosts hate being turned into."

The cable began to move.

"That's telling him, Perry," said Edward. "Keep it up."

"You children don't frighten me," said Skags. "I could squash you all if it suited my fancy."

"Oh, sure," said Perry. "You call yourself a ghost. What a mess you made of that hotel back there. You can't even manage a simple little haunting. I'll bet you could be kicked out of the ghost union for that."

"Keep talking, half-pint. I'll enjoy dealing with you all the more." He released Jennifer to pick off some icicles and hurl them from the girder.

The frozen daggers plunged toward Perry. He stretched out his hands . . . By the time the icicles reached him, there was nothing left of them but a fine mist.

"Is that the best you can do, you out-of-date . . ."

"Anachronism," Jamie whispered helpfully.

"Anasprinism!" Perry declared.

Skags shook his fist at him, and while he did so, the crane swung around on its platform. Then, like a giant pendulum, the cable swung toward the exposed beam.

"Jump, Jen!" Alison called out.

Jennifer had no experience with such feats, but the prospect of staying with Skags was all the encouragement she needed. As the cable passed, she grabbed onto it, wrapping her feet around the coiled metal rope and clinging to it with her arms. The cable swung back past a loading platform, and she dropped heavily onto it.

Skags was not impressed. "Childish pranks," he sneered. "She is not safe yet. Can you guard her day and night? I can act at will. What power do any of you have over me?"

"What they have or don't have is hardly of any importance."

Skags froze. That voice . . . It was one he had thought never to hear again.

"Face me when I speak to you, Mr. Skags."

Skags turned to find a figure dressed in a long calico dress with a lace collar, floating in the air behind him. She was holding a parasol over one shoulder.

"Mrs. Murphy!" he gasped.

"Surprised, Skags? Yes, I suppose you are. You were not known for your foresight. Had you been a bit more clever, I might not have caught you skimming profits from the tavern. But all that was long ago." She looked around at the construction beneath her. "I'm sorry to see the tavern gone. What they're doing here does not seem to be any kind of improvement."

"Why have you come back?" asked Skags, in an oddly deflated voice.

"Surely, you know. I certainly have not returned for my health."

"Leave me alone," Skags whined. He pointed at the Wynds. "They will suffer if you don't."

"Ephraim Skags, you were always a scoundrel, but I trust the passing years have not robbed you of what little sense you once possessed. These children are not my concern. I am not here on their behalf. I am here because you have flouted my curse. You seem to think you are beyond my power." She smiled grimly. "This is not so."

Skags swallowed hard.

"How many years do you have left on your curse?"

"Twenty-seven."

"How would you feel if I started your curse over? I could do it. I *may* do it in any event."

Skags's face was a mixture of horror and defiance. "Don't . . ." His voice was a gnarled whisper.

"I thought that would be your reaction. You're a bully, Skags, but you've got no stomach for a real fight." She paused. "Still, with the tavern gone, I should give you something to fill your time. I must say I am not pleased you had the tavern destroyed."

"I had little to do with that," said Skags. "It was mostly the work of a descendent of mine, a real estate agent. His company arranged the project."

"Really? Well, then, I have a score to settle with him, too. A descendent of yours, you say. Somehow I suspect you deserve each other. What's this worm's name?"

"Ratchet. Horace T. Ratchet."

Mrs. Murphy nodded.

"I believe Mr. Ratchet should be taught to have more respect for historical property. I want you to be his teacher, Skags. That will be your task for the next twenty-seven years. Haunt this Ratchet properly, and we will not need to meet again. Fail to do so, and I will devise a new curse for you. And Skags, should that prove necessary, I promise that you will find this new curse most disagreeable."

Skags hung his head. The thought of being saddled with a new and disagreeable curse was more than he could bear. "Very well," he said, "I will do as you say. First, though, I deal with this girl."

"No!" Mrs. Murphy said sharply. "Enough of your sentence has been wasted already. Do not try my patience further. Get after that man, Ratchet, and get after him now."

The humbled ghost had no choice. Muttering to himself, he slunk away into the night.

"What now?" whispered Alison, once he was gone. "Are we going to have to deal with her?"

Edward prepared himself for the worst.

"No, dear, you're not," said Mrs. Murphy, gently floating to the ground. She steadied herself with the parasol. "My, that was exciting . . . A bit higher than the bus station, too."

"The bus station?" said Jamie.

The shape of Florence Murphy blurred and shifted, leaving the familiar form of Celia Wynd in its place.

"In person," she said.

The children crowded around her.

"How did you do that?"

"Where did you get the idea for those clothes?"

Aunt Celia beamed at them. "Children, children, one at a time. My, that brought back memories. In my youth I was often involved in amateur theatricals. Of course, I stayed away from illusions in those days. They can be somewhat risky. I always had a tendency to blur around the edges. In this case, though, that only helped the effect. As for the clothes, they were just the sort of thing Florence Murphy wore. She favored buttons and tight corsets."

"Your voice was great!" Perry said approvingly. "You sure told Skags off!"

"I was rather harsh with him," she reflected, "but I daresay he deserved it. A more disreputable rascal would be hard to find."

"I'll say," said Alison.

Jamie let out a long breath. "Well, it's over now," he said.

"Over?" cried Jennifer, from the platform above their heads. "What do you mean, over? How am I supposed to get down from here?"

Perry looked up. "Honestly, Jen, sometimes you're such a baby. Just get down the same way you got up, on the ladder."

"Don't be stupid, Perry. I was dragged up here against my will."

"Details, details."

But when she took her last step off the ladder, he was there to make sure she didn't fall.

THIRTEEN

"IS EVERYONE packed?" Aunt Celia asked.

The Wynds were gathered in Aunt Celia's front hall, ready for the ride to the bus station and the trip home. Their luggage was piled on the floor, their coats were buttoned and zipped.

"We're all set," said Edward.

"I'm sorry to see you leave," their aunt admitted. "Next time you'll have to come for a week."

"Do you think we would survive it?" asked Perry.

She smiled. "It would be interesting to find out."

"At least we're not leaving you alone," said Alison. "Henry will make good company."

"It's too bad about his curse," whispered Jamie. "I know he was hoping that his actions yesterday would count for something. Maybe he'll beat it yet."

"Maybe," said Aunt Celia. "We were discussing that just this morning." She cast a glance at the living room where Henry was dusting the fireplace.

Henry looked up. "Excuse me, madam," he said, "would you care to inspect the mantle?"

"Certainly, Henry."

Aunt Celia walked to the fireplace and ran a finger along the top. She examined it for dust. She saw none.

"Henry, this will never do."

"Yes, madam."

"You'll have to do it again."

"As you wish, madam."

"Next week, perhaps."

Perry frowned from the hall. "Next week?" he muttered. "He'd do it again, then, anyway."

"Hush!" said Alison. "Not so loud. All that was for the benefit of the curse. Aunt Celia and Henry have become friends, and so Henry is no longer eager to fulfill his curse. Aunt Celia doesn't know what deed might lift the curse, so she isn't taking any chances. Nothing he does as a butler will meet with her outward approval."

"Oh, I see," said Perry. "Aunt Celia is pre—"

Alison placed her hand over his mouth. "If Aunt Celia chooses to demand perfection from her servants, who are we to argue with her?"

"But what if Oliver Dunstable finds out?" said Jamie. He might come back and—"

"They'll have a showdown," Jennifer finished for him. "If that happens, does anyone want to bet against Aunt Celia?"

Nobody did. One thing they had learned about Aunt Celia.

She was full of surprises.